City of Kings:

THE FURTHER ADVENTURES

OF K. C. JONES

a novel by

Paul Johnson

 The Wessex Collective, 2007

Published by   The Wessex Collective
P.O. Box 1088
Nederland, CO 80466-1088

Web: http://www.wessexcollective.com
contact: sss@wessexcollective.com

ISBN: 978-0-9766274-8-7

The Wessex Collective, publisher of progressive books:

If literary fiction (story telling) is the way that human beings can understand and describe what history feels like, we believe it should be relevant
to universal and historic human experience. We believe also that literary
fiction provides an opportunity to recognize, with significant impact, the
problems of societies as well as individuals. At The Wessex Collective we
are publishing books that demonstrate an empathy for human vulnerability
and an understanding of how that is important to the larger society.

This Book Is For

FRANCES

Great Love Of My Life

1

When Casey reached the corner he looked left, where all the traffic was coming from. There was a light two blocks farther north that must have just turned red because the flow was interrupted there now, but all three lanes in front of him were still thick with cars and trucks traveling between thirty and forty miles an hour. As he stepped off the curb behind the last parked car on that block to wait for the break in traffic that would allow him to cross to the Park side of Prospect Park West, he heard brakes applied and looked back to find that a gray van had come up Tenth Street behind him. The van was a few feet beyond the stop sign now, only six or eight feet away. He couldn't see the driver at all because of the angle at which the bright May sunlight struck the far side of the curved windshield, but he could see the passenger clearly, and their glances even happened to intersect and lock onto each other momentarily. The passenger was a slender man in his late twenties or early thirties, dark-eyed, Eastern-European-looking. Whatever the hell that means, Casey told himself....

Then the gap in the traffic reached Tenth Street and Casey sprang forward, straight across the road in order to clear the nearest lane for the van as quickly as possible. He was on his way to the post office in Windsor Terrace, then to the Fifteenth Street stop on the "F" train, and from there into Manhattan for two Truffaut movies he'd missed back in his dropped-out seventies which were playing this one day only at the Film Forum on West Houston. Then suddenly time and his mind both went into overdrive, as his left buttock was struck from behind with a force that sent him flying forward and downward, into the asphalt, rolling as he turned, hearing himself howl *"No! You ass*hole!*"* as he was dragged beneath the van, meanwhile in the following microseconds thinking very clearly: *That sonofabitch was going straight for the fast lane, and he never once looked anywhere but to the left, at the oncoming traffic, even when he floored it. His front wheel just barely missed me, but he's still turning this way and unless I'm outfuckingrageously lucky, that rear wheel's going to roll right over my hip—*

Then Casey was just as suddenly free and flat on his back in the middle lane, thinking now: *That wheel did miss me somehow, but I'd better get up and out of the way before the light changes again or I'll be squashed like a bug—but hold on, I don't think I CAN get up,* and at the same time: *Where'd that goddamned van go?* and when he craned his neck to look, two deadpan faces loomed close, blocking his view of everything else. One belonged to the van's passenger, the other to a shorter, heavier version who could easily have been the younger one's father. "Are you all right?" they both wanted to know. "Can you get up?"

—*'All right'? Was that a joke?* Casey wondered. "I-I don't think so," he heard himself answering the second query in a squeaky out-of-breath voice; then before he realized what they were up to they'd each grabbed one of his arms and dragged him back over to the west side of the road, where they yanked him nearly upright and leaned him against a parked Volvo station wagon.

"You okay now?" the older man asked.

"...I don't think so," Casey repeated. "...And I'm gonna need some info...on you, and your van...." Reality had assumed a bellows effect, in-out, on-off, empty-full, and the next time it came on he noticed that the older man was gone, or rather was going, trotting across the road toward his van. To get his ID? Maybe—the younger guy was still right there, though. Casey leaned back and gazed upward, at a vast blue sky with a single perfect Eastman-Kodak cumulonimbus cloud in it, thinking, *What a gorgeous day I picked to get knocked down by a truck* and simultaneously, *Now I'll probably NEVER see those Truffauts*...and when he looked again, the passenger was back at the van, too, and climbing into it. *You bastards, you'd better not run off and leave me here!* he yelped to himself, meanwhile fumbling in his fanny-pack for something to write with, and something else to write on, certain he was going to be too late. But the van still sat there, for at least another minute, as he finally discovered the butt-end of a pencil and half a movie ticket *...M...2...8...5...3...1...Y*, he laboriously inscribed, as the van pulled out into the stream of vehicles, and was gone.

✢

So was Casey then, for how long he couldn't tell, before another face appeared close in front his own. A café-au-lait face this time, round, female, fortyish, and concerned. "Did those men just drive off and leave you here like this?" she wondered, and then, "Are you in shock?"

He nodded enthusiastically. —*That's the answer, of course! No problem! I'm just in shock!*

The traffic was in a brief hiatus again. "Can you walk if I steady you? Come on, let's get you across to that bench over there." It seemed a matter of miles, but get there they eventually did, just in time. At the curb opposite the bench a yellow school bus stood parked, filled with more concerned brown faces. It hurt like hell to sit down, his left hip in particular—but come to think of it, lying flat on the asphalt, standing, and walking over here hadn't felt so great, either. Reality was still rushing at him in fits and starts, not necessarily in proper sequence. Now he remembered her first question, as well as the fact that he'd managed to copy the license plate. "They did drive off…but I got the number!" Blinking but triumphant, he showed it to her.

"I wrote it down, too," she told him. "It was five-*one-three*-Y, though, not five-*three-one* like you got it here. But hey, don't you want me to call an ambulance? I've got a cell phone right over there in my bus."

"…That's *your* bus?"

"Well no, not really, but I'm the driver."

"And you saw them hit me?"

"Oh yeah, I saw everything. Boy, those guys are some kinda creeps, to run off like that. I am calling an ambulance. You don't look good."

Casey remained focused on not letting those guys get away with leaving the scene. "…Can I have your name and phone number?"

"Huh?" She had her phone open now and was already punching in nine-one-one. "Hello? Yeah, I want to report a hit and run at Prospect Park West between Tenth and Eleventh. Victim looks like he's gone into shock…Okay now, what did *you* say?"

Casey asked her again for her name and number.

"No, man, I'm sorry, but I can't, I just *can't* get involved. You have to believe me, I can't *possibly* take time off work to go to court. But good luck! I really hope you nail them bozos, they absolutely deserve it!" She climbed up into her bus, closed the door, and drove away, too quickly for Casey even to begin to copy down *her* license number.

✚

Scarcely two minutes later, the ladder truck from the fire station on Eleventh between Seventh and Eighth Avenues clanged to a halt where the bus had been. Several men in big black rubber pants held up by heavy-duty red suspenders climbed out with a big, beat-up-looking first-aid kit, an oxygen tank, and a stretcher. They looked at Casey sprawled there on the bench from a discreet distance, asked whether he was the victim of a hit-and-run, and did he need oxygen, and when he nodded, then shook his head harder, they conferred briefly among themselves—then *they* called nine-one-one, too. "Stay right here," the one with the cell phone told him, "they say there's an ambulance already on the way." Then they all climbed back into their fire truck and it roared off southward, siren abruptly whooping.

✚

The ambulance crew—a red-bearded fat white man, a skinny young Hispanic man, and an Asian woman driver—really seemed to know what they were doing. They had him flat and fairly comfortable on a collapsible gurney with a blood-pressure cuff on one arm, a glucose drip affixed in the other, and most of his pertinent medical history jotted down on a clipboard before the brief ride to Methodist Hospital, between Sixth and Seventh Street on Seventh Avenue, was more than half over. That was where New York's Finest caught up with him, still on a gurney in the hallway, waiting for a free space in the Emergency Room.

The cop who questioned him was a chubby strawberry blonde in her twenties and a too-tight uniform who, Casey learned later, indicated on the form she filled out that traffic was north- rather than southbound on Prospect Park West. She'd also spelled his surname wrong. That hadn't ever happened to Casey before, since his surname was Jones. *Joens* was what she had written, as well as he could make out when he eventually got a copy back from Albany. "Kermit Clarence Jones," he was sure he'd told her distinctly, "but I just use the initials on those first two. I mean, you know, everybody calls me Casey? That's Kay Cee." She hadn't seemed to get that, either, but he'd been too sore and weary to explain it again, and besides, he was more concerned by that time with getting word of his whereabouts to Ru.

2

For at least an hour now he'd been sharing a curtained-off cubicle with a bony, red-faced Irish septuagenarian who reeked of dried piss and cheap whiskey, complained of dizziness and chest pains, and swore he'd been lying there waiting for someone to come take a look at him since seven-thirty that morning. Finally, one of the orderlies who'd peeked between the curtains occasionally (but until now had only responded to their querulous pleas with idiotic grins and waves) actually entered the cubicle and stayed long enough for Casey to press a five-dollar bill with Ru's office number scrawled along the margin into his palm and to persuade him to call her at work: "Don't tell her I got hit by a van, though, she might worry. Just say I fell—that I only stumbled or something, okay?"

Then he added: "And would she mind picking me up here after work?"

Because by then—whenever it was, he'd lost all track—Casey had begun to admit to himself that he might possibly not be able to leave there under his own power (assuming they ever would get around to looking him over, so he *could* leave)...and that his left leg did hurt like a sonofabitch...in spite of his swallowing two large white tablets from a tiny paper cup that a nurse had handed him when he was first wheeled into that cubicle. But those tablets, come to think of it, were probably why everything he looked at now wore a fuzzy purplish halo...

✢

He heard her for a minute before he saw her:

"... Look, I *know* you told me I can't come in here, but as you can see *I am in here* anyhow, so you may as well just tell me where you've put him and save us both time and trouble." That penetrating alto resonated like a viola through the ward. He'd told her once that should have been her name—Viola—but she'd demurred. "Ruby fits me fine." There was nothing literally ruby-like about Ru, but the name did fit perfectly somehow. Casey really couldn't imagine calling her anything else—

A swift division of curtains and there she stood, very much the professional woman in shapely black slacks, Harris tweed jacket and apricot crepe blouse. She'd been his constant companion for a decade already and still her appearance anywhere sent a thrill clear through him, even in circumstances such as these.

"—Casey! What did you *do*? Whoever called me only said that you were here because you'd 'tumbled at work' and then hung up. I was terrified—you weren't up on anybody's roof today, were you?"

"Not today, no."

"Well, what *did* happen? No one out there would tell me Fact One."

"... I was done for the day, and crossing Prospect Park West—"

"Oh *NO!*"

"... It wasn't that bad, Ru, really—"

"Can the soft soap, Jones! Did you get hit by a car or *didn't* you?"

"...Not a car, actually."

"Then 'actually' what was it?"

"It was a van—but it couldn't've gone more than twenty feet, from a dead stop, before it reached me...."

No matter his minimizing, she soon had every salient fact out of him.

"... And then those shit-heads just drove away and *left* you there?"

"Yeah, but I got their license number. And gave it to the cops." Both versions, just in case.

"Good. But what's been happening since you got here? Has an ER doctor seen you yet? Were you X-rayed? Have they called *your* doctor?"

When he signaled a negative to all three questions, Ruby went into action, and within the next half-hour:

1) his GP had been paged throughout the hospital, to no immediate effect;

2) an ER doctor, accompanied by a nurse and two interns, had quickly but quite thoroughly examined him;

3) his gurney had been wheeled to the X-ray section and placed at the head of the line.

"...What about all those poor bastards behind me?" Casey whispered when she bent down to smooth his forelock back from his brow.

"I'll bet they haven't been waiting in here as long as you have."

"*I* wouldn't bet on that."

"All right, then, they're just not as lucky in love as you are."

"No question there."

Shifting from position to position on the gurney and remaining in each as long as the sad-eyed X-ray technician wanted him to was amazingly painful, but luckily Ruby wasn't present to see the expressions on his face, and by the time he was wheeled out again he had them back to something like normal. Somehow she'd gotten the tech to examine the prints immediately and to return minutes later with his answer: "I can't find no break, ma'am."

Back to the cubicle, then, where the Irishman had vanished; conveyed at last to a bed and a bath upstairs, Casey hoped. Ruby chased down one of the interns, who said if there's no broken bone, that's it then, nothing more they could do for him here, the doctor in charge would sign him out.

"What do you mean? How's he going to leave? He can't *walk*!" A few more pithy sentences from Ruby, and the ER staff quickly produced a pair of new wooden crutches that, adjusted to their fullest extent, finally enabled Casey to hobble out to her car.

3

All of the above occurred on the first Friday in May and was followed, for Casey, by a spectacularly miserable weekend. Getting out to any movie was out of the question. His discomfort was so continuous, intense, and distracting that he couldn't even read or listen to music with anything like concentration, let alone pleasure. No position was tolerable for more than minutes, and even with most of the old painkillers lurking in their medicine chest, he only managed a total of seven hours' sleep over the next three nights, half an hour or so at a time, sprawled in the over-sized Lazy Boy recliner Ru had bought him for his sixtieth birthday.

There *was* a break, of course. An MRI ordered by Casey's GP found it on Monday morning. Only a hairline fracture, but it ran straight through the crotch near the top of his femur where the knob that fitted into the pelvic socket forked off the main shaft, and "You wouldn't want *that* snapping off all of a sudden," declared the red-faced orthopedic surgeon called in by the GP. It needed to be reinforced by a long screw and a metal plate, he added, and he ordered that Casey be put into the next available bed and scheduled for operating-room time within the next twenty-four hours.

That was around two PM. At six, Casey was served an unidentifiable but not quite un-ingestible cold supper on a tray in an Emergency Room hallway. At nine, he was at last wheeled into an elevator, then shifted from the gurney he'd occupied since noon to a bed in a darkened double room. He gulped tablets from yet another paper cup and sank gratefully into oblivion, until some hapless intern on the graveyard shift woke him at three-thirty for a rectal exam. Casey told the intern precisely where he could put his Vaselined, latex-gloved middle digit, and the miserable fellow slunk away, never to return.

The surgery finally took place Friday morning (Yes, you read that right) leaving Casey's left hip with several times more empurpled flesh than the accident itself had created, a grisly seven-inch incision closed by a dozen huge stainless steel staples, and all sorts of brand-new pain. By then there had been two different patients in and out of the other bed, with a third freshly installed and already entertaining noisy visitors when Casey was at last brought back from Post-Op. He felt as if he'd been confined in that eighth-floor room beside its sepia-tinted, south-facing window for months already, gazing dolefully down on Park Slope, Brooklyn—his hometown for the past decade—in busy, blowsy, full-blown springtime. If he'd wound up where he was now a week or two earlier, before that ornamental cherry in front of the building exploded, he could actually have seen the entrance to his and Ru's building four blocks away, and their apartment's two tall front windows....

✧

When Ruby had called the local precinct house on Monday, she was switched to a Detective Metcalf who said he had already run the license numbers and driven to the address his computer spewed back at him. Also that the fellow who'd answered the door there had freely admitted he'd "bumped" somebody on Prospect Park West the previous Friday, but he'd stopped and checked and believed the guy was unhurt. The van, it turned out, was registered in the fellow's wife's name and insured for the minimum legal amount, twenty-five thousand dollars plus the medical coverage, and Detective Metcalf had taken down all the requisite numbers.

"Didn't you arrest him," Ru had wanted to know, "for leaving the scene of an accident?"

"If you want me to do that," the detective told her, "your husband will have to press charges."

Ru couldn't quite imagine Casey—a congenital anarchist—

ever doing anything like that, so she said nothing further about it. Meanwhile she'd also been calling around about a lawyer, and found one who not only came highly recommended but would be able to come by the hospital the next evening. When he showed up, Casey asked him whether it was really necessary to press hit-and-run. "If I know anything about this sort of thing," Casey said, "the guy's insurance company will punish him plenty."

"Well, it shouldn't affect the outcome of your lawsuit one way or the other." The lawyer was a local boy, Italian-Irish, with a much better bedside manner than the orthopedist's. Casey wasn't sure he needed a lawyer, but Ruby was, so he acquiesced on this one.

4

Ruby brought him his Walkman, a big box of favorite CDs, paperback mysteries by the bagful, more fresh fruit than he could give away, and the Rochester Big-&-Tall bathrobe she'd given him their first Christmas together. That was when the nurses began getting him out of bed for half an hour at a time, on the second day after surgery. Starting on the fourth day, at ten o'clock someone would take him via wheelchair down the hall to Physical Therapy, where they taught him how to deal with stairs and use a walker. He spent the rest of the time reading mysteries nonstop for somewhere else to put his mind, and even ate a few pears and apples, because Ruby devoutly believed that fresh fruit would heal almost anything.

He didn't mind the sitting up, or the physical therapy—neither activity hurt much worse than just lying there. He didn't even mind the food that much: aside from that first supper, it wasn't bad, and was sometimes almost good. What he *did* mind was not being at home with Ru and free to do whatever he wanted, whenever he wanted to do it.

When Ruby came to visit, all she wanted to discuss was the progress he was making and all the work she'd been doing for him, talking to the police, the lawyer and insurance people, enquiring first about orthopedists and lawyers, then rehabilitation centers. The only topic Casey wanted to discuss was when he could go home.

"Well, you've got to stay here for a full week at least, post-op. But then you'll be sent to a rehab place for another month of intensive physical therapy, or maybe six weeks if I can talk that bitch at Allstate into it."

No Fault was covering his bills, Ru had informed him earlier, which meant the Allstate Insurance Company was. Which meant that Ms. Carmela Palomino-Cruz, who okayed expenditures on his case, was the female canine to whom Ruby referred. Casey thought he understood that much, if not precisely everything that New York State's "No Fault" law might imply.

"Don't do me any favors. Can't I get physical therapy at home?"

"You wouldn't get nearly as much. And without all that equipment."

"I'll never make it, Ru. I'll go berserk. We Scandinavians do that, you know. It's my Viking heritage." Casey's mother being half Norwegian.

"Well, I want you fixed right. In every bit as good condition as you were before. Or *I*'ll run amok. That's my Jewish heritage."

19

"I'm serious. I couldn't take another month of this confinement, never mind six weeks. I might as well be in jail. I can't even smoke a little hooty weed when I feel like it. Not to mention never getting laid."

"Ssshh! I'm just as serious, Casey. I don't like sleeping alone any better than you do, but I'm not having you home until you can get around and take care of yourself. Besides, the whole apartment's a hideous mess."

"It is, huh? I don't recall that it was when I last saw it."

"Yes, well, I haven't had *you* there to keep me from scattering my things all over the place, have I? I can't find *any*thing anymore. And since I come here to visit you every night after work, I never have time to look for what I'm missing."

"Sounds like my fault all around, doesn't it?"

"I didn't say that. At the very least I've got to mop the kitchen floor before you come home. It's unbelievably disgusting."

"It gets that way, unless somebody mops it now and then—but wait a minute: *you*'re going to mop the floor, and I can't come home until it's done? Now I *am* scared. I may *never* get out of here."

"Don't be sarcastic. I know I haven't ever actually done it until now, but *you* can't, Casey, and I couldn't bear your seeing it as it is."

"I won't say another word. Just do it soon."

5

Luckily, at least from Casey's viewpoint, it proved impossible to get him transferred to any of what Ruby had been assured were the better rehabilitation establishments in either Brooklyn or Manhattan before Methodist Hospital's administration concluded its inexorable process of ejecting him from that bed in order to insert someone else, so the option of physical therapy at home had to be reconsidered. Since Casey's surgeon was the old-fashioned sort who didn't think PT was necessary anyhow, at least for anyone "in as good shape as *you* are, for your age," and since Casey himself was by this time clearly contemplating extreme measures to get himself de-institutionalized somehow—and also since Ruby had forced Ms. Palomino-Cruz to confess that Allstate would, in that event, be required to pay for a part-time home attendant...*going home!* was what actually occurred. You can't help but be lucky sometimes, simply because the worst can't happen to you *all the time*, as Casey had long ago learned.

When the appointed day arrived, though, the paperwork necessary to get him released wasn't even begun until he was already decked out in his street clothes and propped up in a chair. So instead of noon as promised, *going home!* didn't happen until four-thirty, when an enormously dreadlocked ambulette attendant wheeled him outside to the curb on Sixth Street. The world out there was extremely large, bright, and loud. Cars and trucks seemed gigantic, as well as deafening. They also appeared to be moving at something approaching the speed of light.

"Watch you' head, mon," the attendant cautioned, as he and the very broad, very black driver each suddenly grabbed a side of the wheelchair, heaved it into the back of their van, and strapped it down.

"What you say, Tent Street? Which way thot one go, mon?"

East, Casey told them, and the best thing to do was to go up to Eighth Avenue, hang a right, then another four blocks later. They did all that with their siren whooping, running the red light at Eighth & Ninth Street. "We due back at *five*," the driver explained, "We a'most on *OUR OWN* time now," as he slammed into double-park opposite Casey's building.

Ruby waved from a front window and ran out to pin back the double doors while they lowered him, wheelchair and all, onto the asphalt. As she pondered whether the chair would fit through the apartment doorway, the driver simply picked up all two-hundred-twenty-five pounds of Casey as easily as if he'd been a newborn, strode inside, and gently deposited him in his Lazy Boy. Ruby had hired Casey's friend Ali to disassemble as far as necessary and transport it from Casey's room to the kitchen, where it now supplanted her rocking chair in the place of honor: the corner by the window overlooking the overgrown backyard. Natty Dread followed close behind with Casey's new walker tucked under an elbow and a receipt in hand for the $75 in cash that Ruby had ready, plus a ten-dollar tip, having been forewarned that ambulance companies *never* wait to get paid by No Fault for trips home from the hospital: the universal policy was No Cash, No Carry....

As soon as the door was locked, they were kissing, licking, and groping. "...I'm too afraid I'll hurt you," Ruby whispered in his ear.

"Don't be," Casey told her. "Doing without *this* has hurt me more than anything..." The black-and-white checkerboard linoleum looked cleaner than he'd ever bothered to get it (the entire kitchen was completely gorgeous to his starved eyes), but Ruby spread a clean sheet for them to slide down onto, and pulled the striped curtains across so the neighbors couldn't watch them, before descending upon him. It was almost like being an adolescent again: immediately upon entry (more precisely, engulfment from above), he erupted.

And erupted. For what seemed like hours.

"...My god, Casey! That was amazing!"

"Wasn't it."

"You're sure you didn't hurt yourself?"

"Absolutely, positively certain."

"But that's what you'd say anyway, isn't it?"

"I suppose so. But you know I'd never lie to you—unless I thought you wanted me to."

"I'm not sure I wanted to hear that..."

⁜

Crawling back up into the Lazy Boy later wasn't easy or painless, but Casey no longer felt like complaining. About anything.

—*Home!* There was absolutely nothing like it, and now at long last he had one of his own. It wasn't necessarily this rent-stabilized railroad apartment, or Park Slope, or anywhere in particular. It was simply wherever Ru happened to be.

6

Dinner that night was takeout, pre-ordered by Ru from Cucina, the excellent Brooklyn (but nearly Upper-East-Side-Manhattan-expensive) Italian restaurant on Fifth Avenue, where they usually celebrated their wedding anniversary.

"I thought we should celebrate your homecoming," Ru said, just a touch defensively.

"A sweet thought," Casey said, "But I would've been as happy with spaghetti putanesca from Aunt Susie's, across the avenue." Then, much as he wished he wouldn't/knew he shouldn't, he couldn't stop himself from asking, "How much did this spread set you back, anyhow?"

"That's really none of your business—it's a present."

"Look, Ru: I'm probably not going to be earning much for another half or three-quarters of a year. And this means we're not going to be able to live the way we have been, never thinking twice about doing or buying anything we feel like."

"You mean *you're* not. But then, you never did. I'm always the one that suggests spending money. And even so, I don't do it anymore like I used to, because I'm always afraid you'll insist on splitting the bill, even though it hurts you like being drawn and quartered to part with each and every penny."

"Okay, I'm a tightwad. You knew that before you married me."

"You're *not* a tightwad—I know very well why you insist, and why it hurts. We've even discussed it a few times."

"You're referring to the fact that I have allowed myself to wind up in a position of economic dependency on the woman in my life at the time—more than once—and it never failed to poison the whole relationship."

"Unless you've been holding out on me, that's only happened to you twice. That's hardly a number to go spinning generalities from."

"I'm not spinning generalities, I'm being very particular. Twice was enough to teach me a lesson: I'm never going to allow it again, and absolutely not now I've finally found you."

"That's very, very sweet, but you're being an ass. You'd barely

finished taking six months' worth of your 'retirement,' as you call it,"
(Casey having appropriated the term and practice from McDonald's
Travis McGee) "to start another book, so I'm sure your savings
account was still barely three figures when those creeps ran you
down. So how are you planning to split expenses with me for the
next six to nine months?"

"We'll get a notebook, and you'll have to write down all your
expenditures on our or my behalf. When I'm making money again,
I'll pay you back."

"Casey, that's crazy. You'll never catch up, so you'll never feel
you can take time off again to write. We got married, remember?
We're partners now, life partners. Your problems are mine, and vice-
versa. Besides, I've been making pretty good money lately. We'll be
okay; I'll just buy fewer clothes for a while. Meanwhile, enjoy your
osso bucco."

Casey sincerely tried to; but then he noticed an odd scratching
sound. He couldn't be sure where it was coming from, but it persisted,
and grew louder. "What's that?" he asked.

"What's what?"

"That scratching noise." Which was suddenly joined by another,
much louder, very different sound. Casey could make a fair guess at
the origin of this one. "Is that a cat?"

"Umm, yes—but just a very little one."

"That makes it okay? I thought we agreed, No Pets? Certainly,
none as unilateral acquisitions?"

"Casey, wait a minute, I'll explain. But believe me, when you
see him—"

"Which is now about to happen, I suppose."

"Yes." Ru stood and went to the closed door that separated the
front and rear halves of the shotgun apartment. He couldn't see
what entered as she opened it a couple inches—their bed blocked
his view—until it rounded the corner between the bathroom and rear

outside door, and poked its head past the bureau. When it spotted Casey it went no farther, just stood there staring at him unblinkingly. A half-grown orange tiger with white feet, bib, tail-tip and whiskers, and tall pointed ears.

"Okay, I've seen him. Now what?"

"Well, you remember that falling-down house around the block on eleventh where that white-haired woman lived, with all those cats?"

"Yeah?"

"Well, it turned out she died in there a week or so ago. So when somebody found her, the ASPCA…"

"Came and gathered up all the cats?"

"Well, not quite all. This one and a couple other little ones managed to squeeze out through a crack where an old window didn't quite close."

"What happened to the other escapees?"

"I guess some of our neighbors took them in."

"Why do you suppose they didn't take him, too?"

"Well, he's very cautious. It took me three days to coax him up on the window sill to drink a little milk out of a saucer."

"Are you sure it's a he?"

"That's what Jacky Upstairs said. She went out back through the basement with a piece of bacon, and snared the littlest one."

"If Jacky Upstairs said so, then it's true. But you should know that milk isn't good for male cats. It gives them kidney stones."

"How do you know that? I thought you didn't like cats."

"I don't, particularly. That doesn't mean I can't pick up a few facts about them, here and there."

The cat, meanwhile, was following their conversation like a tennis match, glancing from one face to the other, as they spoke. When there was a pause, he said, "Mrrgnawyro?"

"Great, a talking cat," Casey said. "—Mrrrow? Mrrrowski?"

"Mrrrghghgh," the cat seemed to reply. He moved forward, half of what had been the distance between them, sat down, and raised his paw for a lick, ignoring both humans. He had some scabs and scarring, but looked, if not sleek, generally in robust health. Now he was licking his nuts. Those would have to go...

"Casey? Can we keep him? Just for now, see how it works out?"

"Keep him? That doesn't enter into it. Seems like he's deigned to honor us with his presence, for an indefinite period of time. Just one thing—"

"Yes? Yes?" Ru was bouncing up and down on her toes.

"Who empties the litter box?"

"Ha! I thought you'd ask that. He doesn't use one—he scratches at the window when he has to go, and does his business in the back yard."

"Great, but while we're at it, two more things—he needs a name, and he is never, *never*, allowed up on our bed." They had a very special bed, built by Casey, two feet high for incredible fucking, with access to deep storage equal to two level pickup bed loads of cardboard cartons. "Is that agreed?"

"I thought you named him already," Ru said. "Mrrrower? Mrrrowski?"

"I'll buy that—Mrrrowski he is. A Polish orange tiger. Most appropriate.... But *is* that agreed? The second thing I said, about the cat, and the bed?"

"Oh yes. Definitely."

We'll see how definitely, Casey thought to himself, as he turned back to scrutinize this new feline roommate, just as the cat delivered an indisputable wink in his direction.

This better not get too creepy, Casey thought; he'd damn well better be one hundred percent real cat, and nothing else....

7

After attempting briefly to sleep beside Ruby on their king-sized futon that first night, Casey retreated to the kitchen. He spent the rest of that night in his Lazy Boy, and the two following. The next morning, Thursday, the physical therapist made his first appearance, leaning on the bell while the cat shot out the window into the back yard and Casey finally made it over to the buzzer by the door on his walker.

"I am Mister Amirji—and you are Mister Jones!" the man bellowed as the apartment door slammed closed behind him. He was built like a diminutive sumo wrestler, wearing a three-piece seersucker suit with a white shirt and red polka-dotted bowtie, a towering pale blue turban on his head.

Casey nodded agreement, hobbling behind his walker back to his Lazy Boy beside the kitchen window.

"Tell me, please, Mister Jones: where do you sleep at night?"

"Well, so far, right here in this chair. It's just too damned painful to stretch out flat on the bed."

"Ah, no no no no NO! You *must NOT* do that! Otherwise your hip will heal that way, and you will *NEVER stand up straight again!*"

"I hadn't thought of it like that. I'll do my best." And from that night on, he did. The first few nights were unrelieved agony, but by the middle of the following week, Casey was able to sleep straight through until morning, flat on his back. Ru made no complaint about how loudly he snored lying that way: she meekly stuffed her ears with cotton every bedtime until he was able to go back to sleeping curled on his side, like an enormous embryo and for the most part as silent.

Mrrrowski, however, took Casey's retreat to the bed as complete relinquishment of the Lazy Boy. Whenever Casey left it in the daytime, to use the toilet or get something out of the refrigerator, the cat would leap up there and crouch in his most menacing manner, until Casey made as if to sit down right on top of him.

Mr. Amirji came to the apartment three times a week through July until Casey was able to get up and down the front steps and in and out of a cab, and thus to a physical therapy center near Grand Army Plaza. Casey was sure he must have been a regimental drill sergeant in some former, colonial incarnation, but he was probably what Casey most needed at that point. Certainly, Mr. A was a merciless taskmaster when it came to the half-hour of calisthenics he insisted upon leading at the end of every visit with a bellowed "One! Two! Three! Four! Faster, please, Mister Jones, and harder, much HARDER! ..."

✣

And the Plaza Rehabilitation Center was exactly what he needed for the next couple months: hot compresses followed by intensive and enthusiastic massage of the area surrounding the incision along his left thigh, followed by three-quarters of an hour of rather lackadaisical exercises under the aegis of one of a half-dozen cheerful, mostly buxom lesbians.

By October, Ruby's numerous advisors in the medical world had convinced her, if not Casey, that he needed guidance from someone with a background that focused on the complete physical system. After making a quick but definitely thorough study of the whole sprawling field of physical therapy, she centered upon the school of practice founded by a Swiss engineer/mountain climber named Feldenkrais, who messed up his legs badly climbing (or rather, falling) in the Alps, then was unable to find anyone to help him cure his ills, so he applied his engineering knowledge to the human body, and proceeded from there to devise exercises specifically aimed at particular problems, and spent the rest of his life teaching them.

The practitioner that Ruby found for Casey was a young Polish woman named Kashi Kajinsky, whose office was one narrow room in a narrow steel-and-glass brownstone replacement full of physical and other sorts of therapists just off Second Avenue in the Seventies. It was six blocks from the Lex Line, plus a complicated change from the "F" to the Lex at Fifty-third Street with a lot of steep stairs, but he'd recovered enough ability by this time to do it safely. And besides, he rather missed the Big City across the River, where all the best movies played first, and often, they only played there. He hadn't, at this point, been outside Brooklyn—scarcely outside Park Slope—for nearly half a year.

8

At Ru's suggestion, the first time he went to see Kashi, he took those crutches from the Methodist ER with him, because he wasn't sure he wouldn't need them to fend off rush-hour A-Types who might otherwise knock him over in their desperate attempts not to be late. His first appointment wasn't until 10:30 AM, but even so—there were New Yorkers who behaved like that all day…

The entrance to the building was behind a newsstand, with a

dimly claustrophobic tiled corridor leading to a minuscule elevator, which was empty and waiting for him. He shuffled in, pushed the button for "3," and stood facing the door, resting his armpits on his crutches.

When the elevator stopped at the third floor and the doors slid open, there was another man facing him, just inches away, not quite as tall as Casey but easily twice as wide.

Casey leaned forward, uncomfortably close, but noticeably leftward. The other man did not respond by moving to *his* left.

Casey returned to vertical. The other fellow leaned straight forward, jowly blue jaw first.

Casey raised his right crutch, as an argument, not a threat, but the gesture rendered him less stable, and he was swept aside, as the other man barged into the tiny elevator car and knocked him into the corner by the control buttons.

They stood glaring at each other as the doors began to close, forcing Casey to pivot back to face them and shove his crutch into the narrowing crack. A warning bell began to ring, somewhere below.

"*As*shole!" Casey couldn't help muttering, as the door reopened and he swung himself out into the corridor. "Don't you know what crutches mean?"

"You're the asshole, Stupid!" the other man managed to growl before the door re-closed. "They're gonna make you throw those sticks away!"

✣

That was, of course, the first thing that Kashi did: "Do you really need those?" she demanded, and when Casey shook his head dubiously, she said, "Then don't carry them around and become even more dependent on them than you already are."

She gave him the title and author of a book to buy and bring with him next time, and when he did, showed him three-quarters of an hour's worth of exercises in it that she wanted him to start doing thirty times apiece every day, at home. His appointments with her would be three times a week, and consist of another hour's worth of exercises that required equipment, including fifteen killer minutes on a stationary bike.

At the end of that first session, Kashi had asked whether it would be all right to make his future appointments an hour earlier. In his exhausted condition, he couldn't see why not.

⁜

That had been a Friday. When he came in the following Monday morning, bearing the exercise book, the waiting elevator already contained two women, but the third-floor landing was unoccupied. Then Casey stepped into the waiting room that Kashi shared with five other physical therapists, and saw him sitting behind his *Daily News*: the Ass Hole, as big as life and looking twice as nasty as he had the first time. Casey fell into the most-distant empty chair, yanked the paperback Stuart Kaminsky he was currently reading out of his coat pocket, and buried his nose into it as deeply as possible.

Gradually he became aware that the young woman behind a little desk at the far end of the room was waving a clipboard and a ball-point pen at him. He walked, with a heavy limp but crutch-less, to her reach and back, and as he did so, he noticed something he'd somehow missed the previous week: there were six doors in addition to the entrance from the corridor, two in each of the other three walls, and each door had someone's name printed on it, followed by various initials. Kashi's was on the left, behind the desk. Meanwhile, Ass Hole smirked and waited until Casey had let himself down into his chair again to say loudly: "Didn't need 'em after all, did you?"

"I guess not," Casey said, opting for a conciliatory attitude he didn't feel for lack of anything cleverer to say. He was damned, though, if he'd apologize for what he'd called the guy last week.

At that moment the door opposite Casey's chair swung open, a woman wrapped to her eyes in yards of slinky fabric slithered out past him, and a brawny Polynesian yelled, "Yo, Mister Baron?— Baronie? Which is it? In any case, come and get it!"

The Ass Hole dropped his *News* on the coffee table and labored to his feet, pausing only in his lurch across the room to clap his massive hand on Casey's shoulder. "That's me: Robert S. Barrone, two 'r's, silent final 'e,' but just plain 'Bob' to you. And you're…?"

"Jones—Kay, Cee, Jones," Casey admitted, grudgingly.

"No kiddin'? Like the brave engineer?" A Wallace Beery slit-eyed grin.

"Nope. No relation." Deadpan.

"Oh no? Gotta see about that…" And Robert S. Barrone made his staggering exit.

✢

On Wednesday, Casey caught an earlier "F" train and beat Barrone to the office by ten minutes. He'd actually considered trying to switch back to 10:30 appointments, just to avoid the guy…and now, when Bob Barrone charged across the whole waiting room to lower himself into the chair beside Casey, he earnestly wished he'd done it.

"How's it hangin', Jonesey?"

"Look, I'd really rather—"

"That I didn't call you Jonesey? Consider it a done deal. It's Casey all the way, from here on out." And he reached out to give Casey's bicep a mighty squeeze, in comradely confirmation. "'N' I'm just plain Bob."

What Casey had meant to say was something more on the order of "Look, I'd really rather not have anything to do with you," but now, gazing into a Beery mug beaming nothing but friendliness, he found any such surly statement impossible. "Uh...okay."

That monumental agreement accomplished, Bob heaved an enormous sigh and asked, as if thousands of lives depended upon it: "You want my *News*? I finished it on the train," meanwhile poking Casey briskly in the sternum with the tightly rolled rag.

"I don't read it."

"You're the *Times* type, I suppose."

"Nope, I kicked that habit long ago."

"So where do you get your news fix?"

"Mostly from the Internet. Or Democracy Now. At last resort, National Republican Radio," Casey replied as if administered a truth serum, wondering all the while why he was opening up so candidly to this colossal creep.

"You must've used to catch Steve Post in the mornings, too, didn't you?" Because Steve it was, on his old WNYC-FM classical music show, who invariably referred to National Public Radio that way: National *Re*public*an* Radio.

And that was a surprise—that Bob Barrone would've listened to that very funny, cranky ex-WBAI-er, Steve Post. Or to classical music at all.

"I read the *News* to learn what real New Yorkers are being told to think. They got some good guys, too—ever read Juan Gonzales?"

No, Casey had never read him, but he'd heard him on Democracy Now, the radio show he co-chaired with Amy Goodman on Pacifica Radio. "And because they got the best sports —don't suppose that matters to you, though."

"No. I hate competitive sports." —Why on earth would I tell this guy that? Casey asked himself. What's happening here?

And at that point they were both called for their appointments.

9

When Casey emerged, limp and dripping, an hour later from Kashi's lair, Bob Barrone was impatiently waiting for him.

"Wanna go get a coffee?"

"Don't drink it anymore."

"Why am I not surprised? So how's about tea? Or hot chocolate? There's a pretty good Greeks' over on the corner of Third."

The Okay was pure reflex. Casey didn't have a movie to see for two and a half hours. And as it turned out, he skipped it, so engrossed had he become in the Saga of Just Plain Bob.

Barrone was a treasure-trove of towering contradictions. His whole family was "mob-connected," as he bluntly put it, except for him and his (now deceased) father, who had been handed a booklet about Malatesta during his first-and-last time in the slammer, forty-odd years before. He took it to heart, and spent the rest of his life preaching the gospel of lawlessness to the habitually illegal. None of them—nobody in his family, anyhow, except for his son—ever bought it.

"You know who that was, though, right?"

"Malatesta? Nineteenth-century Italian anarchist, founder of Syndicalism, if I remember correctly."

"Bull's eye! One absolutely brilliant Italiano, believe me. Came up with the answers to everything that's wrong with society. First name Errico. Last name means 'bad head'—I love that!"

Bob, like his father, chose not to take an active part in his family's many businesses, legitimate or otherwise, he said, but they both had made a comfortable-enough living driving their uncles, aunts, cousins and whatnot around. "Just the more important goombahs, you know—most of the next generation prefers to do their own fender-bending—and I look after their pigeons."

"Pigeons?"

"They all got racing pigeons, young 'n' old. Keep 'em in big cages on the roofs up where we all live, in the Bronx. Race 'em every weekend, and bet like drunken sailors on leave. I just feed 'em, keep 'em clean, report any signs of sickness. I *don't* bet on 'em, don't bet on anything. Gambling's stupid."

Before working with his father, Bob had spent thirteen years attending NYU, including nine as a full-time graduate student. "Then my Great-Uncle Tony finally caught up with me. He called me in one day and said, 'Robert—what're ya gonna be when you finish your education?' I told him, 'I'm not sure yet. I got three master's degrees I could have right now, or anyway as soon as I finish my theses: in Library Science, Philosophy, and American Lit.'" He chews on that for a minute, then says 'Library science? You wanna be a *librarian*?' and I told him, 'I used to think I did, yeah,' and he says, very patiently, 'Librarians don't make any money, Robert—what's more, the Family ain't got no use for one, or for those other things you said, either. You'd be much better off givin' your father a hand with the cars. He's not gettin' any younger.' So that's how I suddenly became a chauffeur. I knew without asking that the Family wasn't going to pay my tuition and living expenses anymore."

Then three years ago Bob's father caught a banana-clip of nine-millimeter lead in the chest that was meant for Great-Uncle Tony. And now Bob's own chauffeuring career had pretty much ended with a totaled Caddy in a head-on that had mashed both his ankles, his right knee, half a dozen ribs and several vertebrae, from neck to coccyx. Once again, the armor-plated Hummer that rammed them was after Old Tony, and once again, he got away with a mild concussion.

Waving imperiously for more coffee, Bob said, "So now tell me about you."

"Why I'm in rehab?"

"That'll do for starters."

"Well, I was crossing a street and got hit from behind by a van."

"Wasn't looking where he was going, was he?"

"I guess not."

"Taking him to the cleaners? You should!"

"You don't find that somewhat out of line with your anarchist principles?"

"Nah, I don't think so. You're really going after the insurance companies, and the whole rotten way it's all set up. This is a very different world from Malatesta's, in a whole bunch of ways, and if he was here, he'd see the differences in a minute and take them all into account. Just for instance, he'd see right away that the corporations run the governments these days, not the other way around—so are you?"

"Am I what?"

"Taking these shit-heads for every nickel you can get?"

"It's not quite that simple. I do have a lawyer. And he's building a case. But the guy I'm sure was driving has slipped out of the picture. It was a father and son, the father behind the wheel. But the pair who showed up for the deposition were cousins, they said, both in their twenties. The son said *he* was driving. And the van's registered in the son's wife's name, carrying the minimum insurance. But the son's in business with the father, and they live in the same house. The business is delivering milk to institutions, like the main Brooklyn Public Library—that's where they were coming from, they said, when they hit me. So they were admittedly on company business, and if they'd been driving the company truck, which has half a mil insurance on *it*, there'd be no question. But that *is* the question now: does the company insurance apply, because they were on company business? That issue comes up before a judge next month."

"Hm. Best of luck on that. But I got to tell you, this whole thing smells about as kosher as ham and shit on Swiss and pumpernickel. Don't you think? Where do they live?"

"Sheepshead Bay."

"Huh. Nobody lives in Sheepshead Bay, at least they don't admit it, they just say Duh, Brooklyn. What's the name?"

"Djokic. Boris, Dimitri, and Shannon."

"Come again? What kind of name is that, anyhow? Russian?"

"Could be, I guess. Eastern European, anyhow."

"Nasty people, some of those guys. Have you checked out the house?"

"No."

"You should. It could tell you what they're worth. Wanna do it now?"

"What do you mean?"

"I'll drive you."

"You're driving? I thought you came down from the Bronx on the train."

"I did. But one of the Family garages is only a five-dollar cab from here. And I can take my pick of what's in there, unless somebody's reserved it."

"I'm surprised you can drive, and would want to, after what you went through."

"I'll quit driving when I'm dead. If then. Most definitely not before."

10

It turned out Bob hadn't yet driven a car since his accident. He was just looking for an excuse to do so, though, and Casey's story provided as good a one as any. But he didn't admit this until he was dropping Casey off at the end of the day. Now, as he chose carefully among twenty Cadillacs, he was still quizzing Casey on anarchism: had he ever heard of a guy named Lysander Spooner?

"If he wasn't the inventor of spoonerisms, nope. Who was he?"

"Just America's greatest homegrown anarchist, that's all. Absolutely brilliant mind. Also one of history's most consistent failures at everything he attempted, from banking to farming to marriage. Yet he took on the almighty Yoo Ess Pee Oh, and drove them to make Congress pass a law expressly forbidding Spooner from operating a mail service of his own—reducing him once again to penury, of course, but at the same time, he bequeathed to all Americans the two- and then three-cent one-ounce rate for more than three-quarters of a century after that: the Pee Oh was that afraid of him, or rather of the specter he'd raised—their having to compete in a truly free economy. He took on the Yoo Ess Constitution, too, in another pamphlet, and totally shredded it as a legal document, line by line…

"I've got a little war of my own going against the Pee Oh in Spooner's honor," Bob continued, as they slipped smoothly into the southbound FDR Drive. "You know what *indicia* are? I didn't think so, nobody does, but we all see them every day. You do know what metered mail is, right? You take this gadget into the Pee Oh, they charge it up with money you give them, plus deposit, and then you run your mail through it, and what gets printed on the envelope, or package—*that's* the indicia. Now, the Pee Oh must've figured there's no need to double-check the gadget they've supplied you that already figured out the postage from how much your mail weighed and where it's going; so when you mail that envelope, their canceling machines just see that it's got indicia on it, and never mind that the date, city, and postage are all wrong, they just automatically send it on its way. So I just cut out all the indicia on the mail I get, and tape them on the next thing I want to mail…"

✢

Casey didn't have the Djokics' address with him, of course, so they'd swung by the Slope on the way. Mrrrowski, as usual, looked distinctly annoyed to be intruded upon in the middle of the day. He actually growled when Casey tried to dislodge him from the Lazy Boy.

"You take that, from a cat?" Bob asked.

"Not my cat," Casey said. He didn't explain, and Mrrowski wouldn't answer when Casey mrrrowed him a couple of times, just to show there were no hard feelings, at least on his part.

"I didn't figure you for a cat person," Bob said. "But then, I don't seem like one either, do I? But I am. Mine's a lady cat. Named after the loveliest human lady who ever lived, Barbara Stanwyck. Spoiled rotten, of course."

Once he'd tracked down the folder with the papers from the lawyer, it didn't take Casey long to find the address. They took the BQE down around the bulging gut of Brooklyn to Sheepshead Bay. Bob seemed to know the area well, but he also had a great set of maps of all five boroughs, Connecticut, and New Jersey. "There's an identical set in every Barrone vehicle," he said, when Casey commented on them. "Somebody had them printed up special as a present for Uncle Sal, who always said, 'Ya gotta know where the hell you're goin' if ya really wanna get there….'

"You know, Malatesta came to New York once, in 1899. He

attended a meeting of Italian and Spanish anarchists out in New Jersey somewhere. Must've been quite a meeting: somebody shot him in the leg right in the middle of it. He went straight back to London, never crossed the Atlantic again. I guess he knew a tough neighborhood when he saw one, and I wouldn't be surprised if Jersey was maybe even tougher back then than it is now."

✢

The Djokics' street was a short, looping, new one, filled with two- or three-year-old townhouses in the five-hundred-thousand to million-dollar range. Theirs was blond brick, with a three-car garage, all doors closed, apartment above. There was a big above-ground swimming pool, a swing set, and a sand box all crowded into the small, fenced-in back yard. No trees or grass back there, toys scattered everywhere.

"So there's grandkids. Old man probably lives upstairs, lets the kids have the downstairs. That's how goombahs usually do it. And I don't have to tell you, these folks're rolling in it…"

The front yard, in contrast to the back, was immaculate, precision-trimmed, bordered with perfect flowers even this late in the year, and definitely untrod upon, maintained by professionals.

Bob was double-parked, motor running, across the street, a few doors before the house. While they sat there looking, a new red Mustang convertible turned in at the far corner and sped toward them as far as the Djokics' garages, where the middle door rolled open for it as it swerved and cruised inside. The top was up on the convertible, and neither Casey nor Bob managed to see who was driving, but they heard shrill, young, insistent voices as the garage door slid shut.

"The wife's wheels, I bet," Bob said. "What's her name, Shannon? A red Mustang fits that like a glove—what the fuck?" Bob said, shifting smoothly into drive and picking up speed as he headed for the nearer end of the street.

"What's the matter?" Casey asked.

"Would you believe it? There was somebody in that farther upstairs window, gawking at us through some fancy binoculars…"

✢

It was time to throw some dinner together when Bob dropped Casey off at home, so that's what he did: mostaccioli with a couple chopped plum tomatoes, sliced Portobello mushrooms, fresh basil, olive oil and a little (for Casey) minced garlic, more of both those last items on a split loaf of Zito's whole-wheat Italian bread, and a bag of pre-washed mixed greens mostly for Ru, who was trying to eat less of his pasta dishes. He moved her row of Annie's Dressings from the refrigerator door to where she could easily choose one, got out the cheese mill and made suitably sized pieces of a well-aged chunk of Romano. By the time he'd set the table the water was boiling, and Ru was unlocking the door.

"How was your day?" he asked.

"No worse than usual," she said, disemburdening herself of her bags, umbrella and briefcase into the Lazy Boy. Mrrrowski never seemed to mind *her* doing things like that, he just made room, accepted some gentle scratching behind the ears and went back to sleep. Later Casey would shift her things to where they belonged, and in the morning she'd demand to know where they'd gotten to. "How was yours? What did you see?"

"Interesting. The Djokics' house."

"That's a movie? Never heard of it."

"No. The Djokics—you know, the people who hit me. I saw their house, palace rather, out in Sheepshead Bay."

"How'd you do that?"

"I got a ride in a black Cadillac with a fellow rehabber—the one I told you about, in fact, the Ass Hole. I have a better name for him now: Just Plain Bob. A pretty interesting guy. A mixture of anarcho-syndicalism, NYU, and Sopranos—the TV series, I mean. That's the part with access to whole underground garages full of Cadillacs, all sizes, mostly black."

"Sounds interesting. You're bosom buddies now?"

"He seems to think so."

"So what did you learn about the mysterious Djokics? Besides that they live in a palace?"

"Well, it's not really a palace. It's just pretentious and cost a shit-load of money. As Bob said, they're obviously rolling in it—the green shit. And clearly they could afford to pay me for my time and trouble."

"And near dismemberment! Excruciating pain! Intolerable suffering! Not to mention extensive damage to *my* peace of mind!"

"Yeah, yeah, all that stuff."

"So why are they being so stinky about it?"

"Don't know why. Or why they're so paranoid."

"Paranoid?"

"You know, I told you about their switching drivers, and today somebody, the father most likely, was studying us while we were studying them—through binoculars."

"That is kind of creepy. I hope you got the hell out of there as soon as you noticed that. And I'm glad you weren't in *my* car."

"That's a thought."

There was another thought, too, that could and should have come behind that one, but Casey didn't think it until much later: if any one did make a trace of the license on that Cadillac, they'd either hit a very paranoid-making blank wall, or, if successful, they'd learn that it belonged to a fairly infamous Italian mob family in the Bronx.

11

Bob's first words upon their next meeting in the physical therapists' waiting room on Friday morning were: "We've gotta talk."

Casey looked a question.

"Not here. After our appointments. Meet you at the same Greeks', okay? Gotta feed a meter first."

Casey limped over to Third Avenue when Kashi was finished with him. Bob was halfway through a whitefish salad on toasted garlic bagel when he got there that smelled incredibly delicious. "Can I have one of those?" he wanted to know.

"That was the last of the whitefish," Bob said.

The middle-aged man behind the counter shook his jowls in doleful affirmation. "The garlic bagels, too."

"Bet you'd never guess what my Uncle Tony said to me last night."

"You'd win, if I'd ever bet."

"He says, 'So what the fuck were you up to out in Sheepshead Bay the other afternoon, Robert?' He always calls me Robert, never Bob. He's like that with the whole family: 'Ya want respect, ya gotta give respect,' he always says. I say, 'Nothing in particular, Uncle Tone. Just looking at some real estate.' He says, 'Don't lie to me, Robert,' and I say right back, 'Would I lie to you, Uncle Tone? Have I *ever* lied to you?' and he says, 'At least a million times, ever since ya started talkin'. Just don't go back there again, okay?' When he says something like that, I know he just is *not* going to tell me what it's about, so I don't even ask."

"What do you think it's about?"

"I don't know anything for sure, but I'd almost bet real money that jerk who was scoping us out with those binoculars the other day got the license, and might've got a make on it somehow. Whenever that happens, to any of our cars or trucks, Uncle Tony gets told about it, and who the hell it was."

Casey had no idea what to make of that information. He signaled the counterman for a hot chocolate and a pineapple Danish.

"Whoever it is, it's somebody Uncle Tony would rather not mess with. And there aren't too many persons that fit that description in these five boroughs. Or Jersey, either."

Once again, Casey came up with nothing by way of reply.

"You know what that does to *me*, don't you?" Bob asked.

"No, what?"

"Makes me goddamn awful curious, that's what. I *gotta* know who that person *is*."

"You do? Well, I'll tell you what it makes me: It makes me think your uncle must have had some very good reasons for that piece of advice, and I think we should be grateful for it, and follow it."

"Come on, Jones—where's your sense of adventure?"

"I'm not sure I ever had such a thing, but if I did, I permanently mislaid it when I finally found Ru. And I don't intend to ever do anything that might impair my chances of climbing into bed with her every night for the rest of what I sincerely hope will be a very long and otherwise very quiet life."

"Look, Casey, I went to a good deal of trouble last night lining up wheels that nobody'll ever trace anywhere. With tinted glass all around that those binoculars will never see through. And it's parked barely three blocks from here."

"Well, I'm sorry you went to a good deal of trouble on what you may have thought was my behalf, but after what you told me about your uncle, under no circumstances am I going back to Sheepshead Bay with you."

"Well, sheesh. Where's your cojones?"

"Right between my legs, where they belong. And now, if you'll excuse me, I've got a movie to catch across town in forty minutes."

⁂

When Casey got home that afternoon, he was surprised to find Ru seated at their round oak table, sipping a cup of Good Earth tea. "Well, hello, Beautiful! What's up?"

"Nothing much. Had a one o'clock dentist appointment, and then I decided it was such a lovely day that I should take the rest of it off."

Gradually, awareness of another difference in their setting seeped into Casey's consciousness. "…So, where's El Gatito?"

"Mrrrowski? At the vets'. Borrowed Third-Floor Jenny's cat carrier. Bumped into her out by the mail boxes, she was just bringing back home the kitten she took in. She said it needed worming, so I figured he probably does, too. Then when I got him there the vet said I had to get him fixed, also, and he needs shots, as well —"

"'Fixed'? I didn't know he was broken."

"Oh, you know, like spayed."

"Female cats are spayed. Males are castrated."

"I hate that word—it sounds so brutal."

"Me, too. But that's the word."

"I hope it won't change his personality."

"You mean make him nicer? I doubt it. He might stop spraying everywhere, though. That'd be a mitzvah."

"Is that what he's been doing? I wondered where that smell was coming from."

"Eau de tomcat. Yes, indeed."

"You don't like him very much, do you?"

"Where'd you get that idea? Actually, it's the other way around. He doesn't like me. He wants you all to himself. The way he thought it was going to be before I came home from the hospital and spoiled everything, as he sees it."

"Don't be silly, he's just a kitten. I'm sure he'll grow to love you as much as he does me, if you'll only pet him more often."

"I don't pet him at all. If I ever tried, I'm sure he'd bite me."

"No, he wouldn't! He loves to be petted."

"By you, he does. Not by me."

"Well, he talks to you."

"Only if I speak first. But who knows what he's saying?"

"I know what!" Ru said. "You should go pick him up tomorrow. I could tell he didn't like that place at all, or me leaving him there. If you show up, instead of me, he'll think you rescued him, and be grateful."

"I think you're mixing your species. I've known grateful dogs, but never grateful cats; in my experience, the only emotions they're certainly capable of are playfulness—by which I mean the way they'll toy with a ball of yarn or a wounded mouse—and resentment...but okay, okay, I'll pick him up."

So Casey did that, and he had to admit that Mrrrowski clearly recognized him, and entered the carrier willingly. The cat even spoke first, for once. In fact, he talked the whole way home, presumably about the horrors he'd witnessed and experienced in the vets' office. Casey didn't talk back to him much—he was too deep in shock over the two-hundred-twenty-eight-dollar total on the bill...

"Do you want to split it with me?" was Ru's first suggestion.

"Do I *want* to? Not especially."

"Fine. I'll write you a check for the full amount. And by the way: did they give you a bottle of pills?"

"Matter of fact, yes." He handed them over.

"Will you help me give him one at night and one in the morning?"

"Sure." And he did. Ru elected to hold Mrrrowski, rather than jam the pill so far down his throat he couldn't cough it up. So Casey wound up with the latter task. Ru did as well as she could, but first the cat slipped out of her lap and had to be caught again, which badly frayed all three tempers. On the second try, Mrrrowski simply freed his right paw and raked one claw the full length of Casey's right forearm, leaving a crimson ditch not quite deep enough to require stitches, but it did provoke a scream from Ru, and choice curses from Casey. All ten pills finally went down where they were supposed to go, more or less on their appointed days and at their appointed hours, but by the end of that slice of time, none of the three were on speaking terms with either of the others.

12

Casey didn't think much of it when Bob wasn't there for his appointment on the following Monday, but when he didn't see him on Wednesday, either, Casey was concerned enough to ask the young woman who served as secretary for all half-dozen physical therapists whether Mr. Barrone had called in sick. She checked the book and said No, she hadn't heard from him this week.

"Do you have a number where I could try to reach him? We had a date to…play chess last night," Casey improvised, "and he never showed."

The young woman took a long, meditative look at Casey's face, and, apparently finding nothing untrustworthy there, plucked a card from the row of them at the back of her desk, and penned Bob's name and number on it. She looked up again, even smiled this time. "Do you want his address as well?" A real New Yorker, he thought: they either trust you, or they don't—no halfway measure....

"Yeah, sure, while you're at it."

When he got home that afternoon, Casey tried Bob's number, feeling slightly foolish, expecting him to pick up within a few rings, but it rang six times, and then Bob's taped voice came on, growling, "Not here right now—try my cell, if you're lucky enough to have it—or else leave a message after the bullfrog." It definitely sounded like a real bullfrog, but then there were several clicks followed by a dial tone, as if the tape was full.

Hmmm...now what? Casey was damned if he knew, and more than slightly annoyed. Just supposing that jerk drove out there again, and...and what? Got himself killed, or kidnapped, or...oh, shit! This is crazy, and anything like that is highly unlikely, and...I don't want to feel responsible, and I shouldn't have to, I mean, Christ, didn't I as much as tell him it was none of his business, and didn't his own uncle order him to keep his nose clean?... But I can't help it, I *do* feel responsible—but what the hell *can* I do?

Dinner was just some of the lamb stew he'd made last week and tonight's portions were already thawed, so all he had to do was stroll over to the bakery on Eighth for some soda biscuits to go with it and a berry tart for dessert. While he was out, Ru called to say she had a big mess on her desk to straighten out, and wouldn't be home until nine or ten. So—he was either going to sit around here spinning his wheels for three hours, or.... He looked up the Neighbs on the Internet, it was an 8-plex, and there happened to be an independent comedy he'd missed in Manhattan, starting in eighteen minutes, he could make it easy...

It was a pretty stupid movie, but it did serve the purpose of keeping his mind off Bob Barrone for nearly two hours. On the walk home he had an idea—but Ru was just coming up Tenth Street from the parking space near Seventh Avenue she'd lucked into just as he was walking down from Eighth, so he put it off until after dinner, and then Ru came up behind him while he was doing the dishes afterwards and started feeling him up—it was the first time since Mrrowsky's epic worming regimen—so they wound up making love and he fell asleep directly afterward.

✣

He woke the next morning remembering the idea, though, and as soon as Ru left for work he started leafing through her folder full of notes from when he was in the hospital, and not too far down in the pile, there it was: Detective Donovan Metcalf, with the number. And he was still (or again) on the day shift, and right there at his desk.

"Hi—my name's K. C. Jones, and I don't expect you to remember this, but half a year ago I was knocked down by a van on Prospect Park West. It was a hit-and-run—"

"Which you didn't report as such."

"That's right. I guess you do remember—"

"Not much, but that, I did. Guys who get hit and left are usually pissed off enough to press charges. It's mostly women who don't, sometimes."

"That's interesting—"

"It's probably just a matter of testosterone, you might want to get your level checked. So what about it?"

"Well, the driver didn't show up at the deposition. His son claimed *he* was driving—"

"Can you prove he wasn't?"

"No, I guess it's just my word—"

"That's right. Tell your lawyer, maybe he can use it."

"Then, last week a friend and I drove by their house—"

"No law against that."

"—and somebody at a window was watching us with binoculars."

"Or that, either."

"I know—but Monday my friend said he was going back out there, in a different car, and he hasn't been seen since."

"You know this for a fact?"

"Well, he's not home, and he hasn't been keeping his appointments—"

"Are you calling now to file a Missing Persons Report?"

"No, I wasn't, but—"

"Call me back when you're ready to do that. Not before." And then Detective Metcalf hung up, without bothering to say goodbye.

13

There was no answer on Bob's phone on Thursday, either. Or Friday. And Casey hadn't mentioned any of these developments to Ru; he could well imagine what her advice would be. On Saturday evening she had a party to go to. And she wanted him to accompany her. Somewhere on Staten Island. Somebody she used to work with.

"Fine," he said, though there were few things he would less rather do than sit around half the night watching an apartment full of folks he didn't know talk shop, gossip about mutual acquaintances he'd never met, and get tipsy, while he nursed a straight club soda. "I've got to do something in Queens this afternoon but I'll be back by five-thirty, six, okay?"

"Did you leave me a number, where you'll be?" Ru called from the bathroom. She'd been after him to carry a cell phone for ages. Always asking for a number was supposed to wear him down eventually.

"Uh, yeah, sure…" Bob's name was on the card that the secretary had given him; that would lead him into an explanation of what he was up to, so Casey took the trouble to copy just the phone number onto a Stick 'Em. Then he decided it looked too naked, and cryptic, all by itself like that, so he added the date and time, and stuck it to her purse on the round oak table.

✤

When Thomas Wolfe famously captured the phrase, "Only the dead know Brooklyn," it was no exaggeration, and it's probably even more true today. One wonders, though, what Wolfe ever knew of Queens. "Not *even* the dead know Queens" is the way Casey would've put it, after two and a half hours, three subway trains, and a bus failed to take him where he wanted to go. Finally he asked at an Italian deli and was given an ominously fishy eye, but also very precise directions that got him there on foot in less than ten more minutes. It was a four-story brownstone toward the middle of a block comprised mostly of once-grandiose red-brick apartment buildings over-decorated with concrete doo-dads. Above the whole block, squadrons of gaudy pigeons wheeled and swooped, and cheers periodically erupted from the rooftops.

Bob's was a basement apartment in one of the smaller buildings, entrance three steps down beneath the stone stairs that rose to the parlor floor. The mailbox was crammed with catalogs and circulars. Casey's thumb on the buzzer was answered by a famished howl from the other side of the door: Barbara Stanwyck, he surmised. Peering through the wrought-iron bars over the windows only took his gaze as far as the dusty, varnished, louvered shutters hooked closed six inches beyond the dusty glass. Could Bob be sick or dead inside there? Should he see if anyone upstairs would talk to him, maybe let him in?

Casey turned on his heels to attempt exactly that, but found himself face-to-face with a trimmer, younger facsimile of Bob, in corduroy overalls and a black turtleneck sweater. "Whadda you want?" it demanded, in a cross between a growl and a grunt.

"I'm looking for Bob Barrone."

"Why?"

"'Why?' Why should I tell you why?"

"Because I asked you, that's why. Next thing I'll do is beat it out of you." He looked like he could, too, and not even pop a sweat.

"Look, I've been trying to reach him all week. He's not answering his phone."

"We know. That's because he ain't been home. Whaddaya know about that? Stay where you are." He produced a cell from his overall bib, flipped it open and punched '1.' It was answered immediately. "Rose? It's Ange. I just caught somebody snoopin' 'round Bobby's apartment. Ask Uncle Tone if he wants to talk to him, or should I?… Right now? Okay, on our way."

"Hey, wait a minute—" Casey started to say.

"Look, you're goin'," the man who'd identified himself as Ange said. "Only question is how: walkin', or dragged."

Casey walked. They went around the block to one of the largest of the apartment buildings, where some twenty teenagers either perched on the steps listening to what Casey assumed was music on a monstrous boom box, or gyrated dervish-like to it in the middle of a sort of combination patio and entranceway. They all bore a strong resemblance to Ange and Bob. Ange cut a path straight through them, and Casey followed. Inside the foyer, four guys who all could have been Ange's brothers were playing poker.

"Gonna see Uncle Tony," Ange said to them, and one nodded. "Rose called," he said. Ange prodded Casey into the nearest elevator, and punched the button marked 'PH.'

14

The penthouse occupied half the flat roof of the building. The rest of it was filled with potted trees and flowers, and a well-padded grandstand built against the one solid wall of the otherwise mostly glass penthouse, where all the Venetian blinds were open, revealing a huge, unmade, circular bed, an enormous television set, and a free-standing fireplace. The trees and flowers were being fussed over by half a dozen little blue-haired ladies in double-knit slacks, twin-sets and dainty gloves, while roughly three times that many mostly little, old and bald men in golf shirts and windbreakers stood in the grandstand and cheered lustily as flocks of pigeons flew around the block, while young men on the corner buildings waved bright flags on tall poles. Most of the roofs of the other buildings in the block also held groups of men, women, and children, all adding their encouragement as the birds sailed over their heads.

Ange kept watching one of the old men until he glanced over at the elevator and beckoned; then Ange walked over to him, guiding Casey along by his elbow.

"I'm Antonio Barrone," the old man said, extending his hand and smiling at Casey. "And you are?"

"Casey Jones."

There was a clouded moment while Antonio Barrone wondered whether he was being diddled with; he quickly decided he was not. "You say you're a friend of my nephew Robert?"

"That's right." Glancing around, Casey noticed that only Ange was listening in on their conversation. All of the old men and women were conspicuously not paying any attention.

"Where do you know him from?"

"Physical therapy."

"Mm-hm. When did you see him last?"

"This past Monday."

"And were you the friend who went to Sheepshead Bay with him the previous week?"

"Yes, I was. He said on Monday that he intended to go there again."

"Did he tell you I had expressly ordered him not to?"

"Yes."

Antonio Barrone shook his head. "Isn't that just like him! It was *your* business that took him out there the first time, wasn't it?"

"Yes, it was."

"Why didn't you go with him this time?"

"Partly because someone was watching us with binoculars the first time. And partly because you'd told him not to."

"That sounded like good advice to you, did it?"

"Yes."

The old man sighed. "Why can't I have more nephews like you?"

"I don't know. It seems to me you have plenty of them already who pay respectful attention to whatever you say. It could be you need some like Bob, as well."

Antonio Barrone decided to be amused. "Really? And what use would a confirmed autocrat like myself ever find for a second-generation anarcho-syndicalist like Robert?"

"Well, you know the old Roman tradition of having a slave accompany each returning conqueror on his chariot, and whispering, as the crowds cheered—"

"'Remember, Caesar, thou art but a man.' A lot of good that did the Roman citizens."

"You're right there," Casey had to admit.

The amusement was over. The old man turned to Ange. "Angelo," he said, "Get Young Joseph, Peter, and Louis. I'll tell you all at once what I want when you bring them here."

"What about this guy?" Ange asked.

"He'll be going with you," and then, turning back to Casey. "This shouldn't take long. Would you rather wait up here and learn something about pigeons, or—"

"I'm afraid I've got an engagement this evening. I should be leaving about now—" Casey began to say, but the old man turned abruptly back to Ange: "Leave him with the boys in the lobby until you're ready to go."

"What about the cat?" Casey asked, as Ange grasped his elbow.

"What cat?" both Barrones wanted to know.

"It sounded like there's a very hungry cat in Bob's apartment."

"You've got a passkey, don't you?" Antonio Barrone asked Ange, who nodded. "Take care of the cat on your way, then—you should've noticed and done that days ago."

On the elevator back down, Casey said, "Look, I'll need to make a phone call."

"When I go back up with the other guys, I'll ask him if that's okay," Ange said, not unkindly.

15

While he was waiting for Ange to come back, Casey taught the boys in the lobby to play the only poker game he remembered, from Boy Scout camp: Piss-in-the-Sink, an X-rated version of Spit-in-the-Ocean. They lost interest, though, when he refused to play for money. "Gambling's the only vice I've never found even the least bit enticing," he told them. "Maybe I just don't care about money enough. If I've got ten bucks in my pocket, the last thing I want to do with it is risk it in an attempt to turn it into twenty." That's not the point, they all argued: what you're really trying to do is take the other guy's money away from *him*...

Ange was back in half an hour with three more semi-facsimiles, these in their early twenties. They were up on the roof only five minutes.

"What about my phone call?" Casey asked when they re-appeared.

"It's okay as long as I listen in," Ange said. "We'll use my cell. What's the number?"

"What time is it?"

"Six-forty." Casey gave him Ru's cell. She'd be on her way to Staten Island by now. "It's ringing," Ange said, and when he heard Ru say "Hello?" he passed the phone.

"Hi," Casey said, "Where are you?"

"Approaching the Verrazano Bridge," she said, clearly madder than hell. "And just where in God's great creation are *you*?"

"Look, I'm really sorry I'm late. I got hung up—"

"On *purpose*! You did it *ON PURPOSE*!" She said it so loudly that Ange grabbed the phone back and said: "No he didn't, lady, it was really beyond his control."

"Who the fuck are you?" Ruby demanded, in astonishment.

"I'm the hang-up he got hung up on, you could say. But not for very long. Just gimme the address, I'll deliver him wherever you'll be within two hours, I promise," Ange told her, digging a pad out of his pocket, reaching for the nearest proffered pen. "...Which end of Staten Island? ...West of Todt Hill? Fine, thanks, I'll find it."

There was a black Caddy Escalade waiting for them outside the building. "Wow, these things are just as ugly inside as out," Casey remarked, as they all climbed aboard, Ange driving. No one disagreed.

They took the BQE and were lucky there was very little construction that weekend. It only took three-quarters of an hour to get to Sheepshead Bay, and another fifteen minutes for Casey to find the Djokics' street. The house was dark except for a television screen in the front downstairs window. Ange drove back to the last pizza place they'd passed and sent Pete in to buy the quickest big pie he could talk them out of, a six-pack of Schlitz and another of Pepsi. Then they drove back to the Djokics', where Lou took the pizza up to the door and leaned on the bell. Finally it opened.

"What I thought," Ange said. "Baby-sitter." The teenager shrugged, grinned, pouted, and showed off her pointy little boobs. Lou nodded repeatedly, shrugged, scratched his armpits, lit her a cigarette. Finally he came back to the car. "They all went to the movies, mom, dad, 'n' grandpa. She doesn't know which one, or when they'll be home."

"So we'll check out the neighborhood 'n' keep checkin' back here," Ange said. "Meanwhile break out that pie 'n' open me a beer, I'm fuckin' starved. By the way, what is it?"

"Pepperoni, pineapple 'n' anchovies, what else?"

They made short work of the provisions as they prowled the narrow streets, looking intently for, as Ange put it, "anything out of place." It was Casey who first spotted the 'seventies Pontiac parked in the middle of a muddy construction site. It was the tinted windows that clued him. Bob had mentioned them.

Ange parked fifty yards away and sent the three younger men to puddle-jump and investigate. They were barely halfway there when they heard the banging. Pete spotted a crowbar dangling from a sawhorse and used it to jimmy the trunk lid. And there lay a furious, and very surprised Robert S. Barrone, kicking away at the rust spot on a wheel-well. He was also quite disoriented, but Casey and Ange eventually gathered that he'd only been in the trunk for a matter of hours. Before that, he'd been chained, blindfolded, to a pillar somewhere—presumably in the Djokics' basement.

They made Bob as comfortable as they could on the back seat of the Pontiac. The keys were in the ignition, and Pete and Joey would drive him back home to the Bronx in it, stopping on the way to clean him up and feed him, while Ange delivered Casey to Staten Island after dropping Lou at the Danovs' to see what more he could learn. The baby-sitter, it turned out, had invited him to come back and keep her company when he was done supposedly delivering pizzas.

✤

The Staten Island party, in one of a long row of fake Tudors, looked every bit as dead as Casey had feared—Christ, were they actually playing *Fleetwood Mac* in there?—but Ange had an idea for waking it up: "Why don't you go ask your lady friend if anybody would be interested in some truly killer sinsemilla? I can donate a lid to the cause."

"Tell you what," Casey proposed, "since I'm late as hell already, let's you and me do up a quickie before I go in." And after that, it didn't matter: Ru took one look at both of them as they came through the front door, and came down—or rather, Up—with one of her legendary contact highs, and the three of them soon had everyone else there livelyin' up theyselves to Bob Marley and passing 'round the spliffs until, at two AM, one of the neighbors finally called the cops.

Ange, Casey, and Ru had all gone their own ways long before then.

16

Sunday Ru and Casey slept late, as usual—or anyhow, as late as Mrrrowski would let them. At nine A.M. he started leaping up onto the foot of their bed, launching loud speech after speech, until Casey sent him flying again with a well-aimed kick from under the covers. Ru, for once, didn't come to the cat's defense; she'd pulled a quilt over her head and lay rolled in a ball, as close to the wall as she could get. At nine-twenty Casey gave up, got up, and dripped up a pot of fresh-ground Chiapan coffee (they'd both officially quit that drug, but Sundays like this one were possible exceptions)—the smell of which was what finally got Ru up, as church bells were ringing for ten-o'clock mass.

"...So what was yesterday all about, anyhow?" she wanted to know, after her second cup. "I mean, what kept you from coming home when you said you would?"

"I'd better warn you: it's a long story."

"I figured it would be. That's why I didn't bother you for it when we got home last night."

"Ha! You weren't even conscious when we got home last night. I had to double-park, drag you in by your armpits, toss you on the couch, and then go find somewhere to park that pathetic gadget you call your car. That took me most of an hour, and while I'm thinking of it it's between Fifth and Sixth on Thirteenth, and you were still snoring away when I got back here."

"How many times do I have to tell you—*I do not snore!*"

"My Dearest Love, *everybody* snores when they lie in certain positions. As for instance, flat on their backs, arms and legs spread wide—" He demonstrated as well as he could, in a chair.

"I've never slept as immodestly as that in my entire life— but you're just trying to avoid telling me what all that was about yesterday, aren't you?"

"No, I'm not, but I'm still not at all sure myself what actually happened and won't be until I've talked with Bob. I hope he's going to feel well enough to come to rehab tomorrow."

"What's he got to do with it?"

"Well, Ange—you do remember Ange from the Staten Island party, don't you?—and three other young Barrones and I all had to go out to Sheepshead Bay and rescue Bob."

"Rescue him from what? Or whom?"

"From the Djokics, I guess."

"This does sound like a long story—complicated, anyway."

"Much too long and much too complicated—for a gray, drizzly Sunday afternoon, certainly."

"Is it already Sunday *afternoon*?"

"I'm afraid so."

"Then how about brunch at Dizzy's Diner? My treat?"

"Twist my arm…"

✢

There were four messages on the machine when they returned, replete and toting a bulging kitty-bag, from Dizzy's. All of the calls were from Bob, and all of them said the same thing, the only variant being the amount of rude language they also contained: "*Where are you? Call me!*"

Casey did that, only to hear: "Stay there! I'm on my way!"

Bob rang the bell barely half an hour later. "I thought you'd want to hear the whole story. Well, not the *whole* story—no telling yet, what the hell that is—but at least I can tell you everything I know, as of now.

"But first, tell me, are you guys hungry?"

"We're stuffed—and Mrrrowski's clearly not into sharing his bagful of goodies."

"Well, can I get anything delivered around here? I mean, besides pizza? That's all they fed me, the whole frigging week!"

"Here, try Dizzy's," Ru said, discovering their menu beneath the cat bag. "They might still be delivering. Just ask what they've got left," dialing for him. "They close in twelve minutes, but they're only a block and a half away."

"...It all sounds great! I'll take your 'Rockefeller Ruben,' then, with a double order of home fries, 'n' your biggest ice-tea. 'N' that crab-apple-raspberry-rhubarb cobbler, a la mode. Make that double a la mode, okay? Be here in less than fifteen minutes, the delivery guy gets whatever's left from a five and a twenty."

✢

"...So I moseyed on out there Monday afternoon. In that Pontiac."

"That much we guessed."

"Well, it's important, because I don't remember anything from then until I found myself blindfolded and chained to a damn concrete pillar, two feet or so square. And then nothing until I came to last night in that trunk."

"Tell me something," Ru said. "Were all your windows closed, after you reached the Djokics'?"

"Yeah, why?... Well, it was pretty damn warm in there, all that dark glass, so I guess I did open the driver's side window, but that wasn't facing the house, see?"

"Somebody hit you in the arm somehow with a hypodermic, though, or a tranquilizer dart. Same thing when you were chained up," she said, and sure enough, she found two pin pricks in the middle of small bruises on his upper left arm, one almost healed, the other more recent.

"Where'd you come up with that bizarre idea?" Casey wanted

to know.

"Where do you suppose?" she asked. "In some dumb book or other."

"That's cheating."

"How so? You do it all the time."

"Well, okay," Bob said, clearing his throat and downing the last of his ice-tea. "I guess that clears that up." It also, though he'd never admit it, left him with very little else to tell. "…The blindfold? It was like yards of sticky gauze, wrapped all the way around my head. It pretty much stopped me from hearing anything, as well as seeing. When they wanted to tell me something, they'd come up real close to say it. I still had it on when I woke up in the trunk of that Pontiac…. Who were they? How the hell should *I* know? They were guys, definitely, young-sounding, I think just two different ones. Feeding or checking on me, just one at a time, but there were always two when they took me to the toilet. Which wasn't very often. They'd drop my pants, push me down on the seat, chain one wrist to a pipe, tell me to hurry up…"

"Always pizza, you said; could you recognize the chain?"

"Chain? The one I was tied up with?"

"No, the brand of pizza! Was it always the same toppings?"

"It was always cold and greasy, I'll tell you that much. And just two slices at a time. Otherwise, I couldn't say for sure. Native Brooklyn pizza."

"Anything to wash it down?"

"Yeah, just water. In a plastic cup. Tasted like it came out of a hose."

"Anything else you can remember? Anything they said? Accents?"

"No particular accents. Sheepshead Bay, I guess. And they never said more than was necessary. The only good thing I can think of about them is, they did keep me chained loosely enough around the pillar so that I could slide down to sit on what felt like an old sofa seat, leaning my back against the pillar. So I was able to sleep. Some, anyhow."

"Did they gag you?"

"Yeah, at first—until the first time they fed me. Then they made me promise, no sounds above a whisper, or they'd put it back on and I'd get no more food or water."

"So you were probably somewhere where you could be heard by some one who didn't know you were there."

"Probably—but I was in no position to gamble on that."

"No, of course not. I don't blame you a bit for cooperating."

"Well, thanks a bunch."

"I'm sorry. I didn't mean that the way it sounded."

"Ha! You made me feel like a collaborator. Believe me, you have no idea what it's like, to be helpless like that, unless you've been through it."

"I'm sure I wouldn't, I mean, don't," Casey said, and he meant it, though he couldn't help remembering a situation he'd once been in, Upstate, with a couple of old friends: *nothing hurts like being completely helpless...*

17

"So now what are you going to do?" Ru asked.

"...Do? ...Now?" Bob wondered, when he realized the question was aimed at him.

"No, I mean, when you report this to the police?"

"Huh? Report *what* to the police?"

"What they did to you."

"What *who* did to me?"

"Don't you see, Ruby?" Casey put in. "There's nothing to report: no what, no where, no who, no why. Nothing even begins to make any sense, and even if it did, even if you could point out possible reasons for any part of it, you couldn't prove that any bit of it happened—it's all in Bob's head, or it might as well be. Your Detective Metcalf wouldn't sit still for two seconds of this folderol."

"*Who*?" Bob was totally at sea at this point.

"Never mind," Casey said. "A perfect crime. Perfectly senseless, utterly unsolvable. Why did somebody—at least two somebodies—kidnap this man, chain him to a concrete pillar somewhere, feed him stale pizza for the better part of a week, and then suddenly transfer him to the trunk of a decrepit Pontiac in the middle of a construction site in darkest Sheepshead Bay? Did they once say anything implying motive?"

"Nope, nothing of the sort."

"Did they, in fact, ever ask or tell you *any*thing?"

"Once again, I have to say 'Nope!'"

"Did *you* ever ask *them*, 'Why are you doing this to me?'"

"Well, they never really gave me a chance to ask questions."

"Okay, but surely you must have wondered, lying there in the dark, 'Why *me*? Why are they doing these things to *me*?'"

"Oh, sure, practically the whole time."

"And what conclusions did you come to?"

"Only one, really: that I was god-diddly-damned if *I* could figure it out."

"And, just supposing you were the sort of guy who would ever tell the cops anything, is this the sort of conclusion you would run down to the precinct house to share with the boys?"

"As a matter of blunt, brutal fact—nope, not in a frillion friggin' years."

"Well, then," Ru persisted in asking, "what *are* you going to do?"

"I'm afraid I'm still god-diddly-damned if *I* know—but rest assured, I sure as hell am gonna do *some*thing!"

"Ah!" Casey said, "you see, that's precisely where people always go wrong; you should—we all should— decide none of this ever happened. Because there are bound to be reasons—and none of them will be half as clear and satisfying as this moment of total, perfect ignorance. They're also liable to entail a great deal of pain and sorrow. Arriving at them could, I mean…"

No one could argue with that.

✢

Further discussion at the Third Avenue Greeks' the next day after PT was a foregone conclusion. Bob began it by saying, "You can tell that Glorious Ruby I was as good as my word: I sure as hell did *some*thing when I got home last night."

"And what did you do?"

"I downed most of a pint of bourbon, and then went and bearded Uncle Tone in his penthouse. 'I'm sure you got a full report from your Myrmidons,' I said. 'After all I went through last week, don't you think I deserve to be told at least the gist of whatever it is that you knew that caused you to tell me not to go back out to Sheepshead Bay?'

"'I don't think you deserve anything but what you got,' he told me, 'or worse. When the fuck are you gonna learn, Robert, that I don't talk just to hear my golden voice?'

" 'Well, maybe I got off on the wrong foot a little bit a moment ago there, Uncle Tone,' I told him. 'What I meant to begin with was some heartfelt apologizing for not taking your advice.'"

"'That wasn't "advice," Robert,' he says. 'That was a pretty clear order, it seemed to me. And you disobeyed it. Now you want me to take pity on you and tell you things I didn't want to tell you before. Does it make any sense, that I would do that? Why should I? Why should I even speak to you, after the way you behaved?'"

"'Because you're my Uncle Tone, 'n' you know I really respect you more than all the other damn Barrones put together—'at which point he starts to lose it a little bit, almost shouting, 'Is that any way to speak about your own family? Let alone it's *my* family, too, you insignificant roach turd, you!'"

"I suppose it went on like this until he threatened to have somebody toss you off the roof," Casey couldn't help interjecting. "So you never learned anything, did you?"

"You're almost right, but not quite. It did go on for quite a while longer, and he did threaten me with being thrown off the roof—by him, personally—but I did finally get him so pissed off that he let something slip. I now know who it is—who's behind those Djokics, and why he didn't want me messing around there. Well, no, not *who*—but I do know *what*."

"So give—what's what?"

"The government—the federal-You-Ess-fucking-Government! That's what."

"Just how did he let *that* drop?"

"Never mind—I mean, it wouldn't mean anything to you, without the context. And no fucking way I'm giving you the context."

"Okay, I'm not sure I'd want it, anyhow."

"No, you wouldn't. Believe me."

"I believe you…but did he perhaps give any indication of what branch of that government it might be? I mean, as we both know well, it's a very large organization. With its hands, and feet, and everything else, into all sorts of things."

"Is it ever."

"So—did your uncle…?"

"No. He did not elucidate."

"So we're in effect no further along than we were already?"

"That's an awfully negative way to put it, Casey. But in effect… yeah, not too much further, anyhow…."

"So okay, I'll gladly tell Ru that you did something. Then we can pretend it never happened."

"*You* can, if you want. I'm still god-diddly-damned if *I* can."

"Realistically, what can you possibly do?"

"I don't know yet. But, Casey, I'll think of *some*thing. Maybe not today. Maybe not next week. But *some*day! And you better believe it!"

18

Xmas was coming. Or Christmas, whichever you prefer. Casey had never had any preference in the matter. He couldn't see that the day had much to do with Jesus Christ anymore, if it ever had—and quite clearly, Dionysius and several other deities had occupied that approximate position on the calendar long before the Nazarene. Of course, there didn't seem to be any connection to X, either, unless you claim it's really supposed to be the Greek letter Chi, in other words, JC's last initial, in Greek. He'd once heard a Born-Againer argue that xmas was a terrible, in fact a Devilish thing to call that day, because X is the unknown quantity, and we all know what Christ is, Christ is Love...but that argument seemed a bit Jesuitical to Casey. As far as he was concerned, before he met Ruby, the twenty-fifth of December was merely one of the two most difficult days in the year to stay sober—with the other following it just six days later...

But Ru changed that. Now the twenty-fifth of December was The-Second-Day-In-The-Year-He-Had-Better-Have-A-Beautiful-Present-To-Give-Her,-OR-ELSE! The-First-, etc., was her birthday, and while he had always had trouble remembering his sons' or anyone else's natal date, including his own, this particular day—April third—was indelibly engraved in his mind.

But during the first few years of their being together, the obligations of those two days had sent him into a panic that had lasted most of the year. Now, blessedly, there was OTTO, down near the end of their block, at Seventh Avenue. OTTO was a small, très-chic, if cryptically named gift shop, which carried some women's lingerie and blouses and dresses, a little bit of jewelry, a few household items, and a few toys. All chosen by Annette Englander, with her unflagging good taste. Annette was German-born, as slender and as timelessly fashionable herself as a fourteenth-century Flemish madonna, as different physically from Ru as any other woman ever could be, but every year now, out of friendship for both Ru and Casey, she selected several items—most often spellbinding nightwear—for Casey to make the final, token choice among, and whichever it was, it always seemed just right.

What a load off his mind! All year long!

But here it was, December already, the seventh in fact, the Day-That-Will-Live-In-Infamy, six weeks after that last conversation with Bob, and he hadn't even gotten around to checking in with Annette, to see what she'd put aside for him. So he was tying up perhaps as many as half a dozen pieces of her merchandise, and would be buying only one. Well, he'd take care of that right now, on his way to meeting Ru at BAM (that's the Brooklyn Academy of Music, to all you outlanders) for soup and a sandwich and an early screening of *Taxi Driver*....

It was a few minutes past five, and as dark out there on the street already as it ever gets in Park Slope, Brooklyn; or maybe even somewhat darker than usual, since the street light directly in front of their building was out. And there was the usual impatient pile-up of cars at this hour, all in frantic search of a parking space. There was also a light snow drifting down, frosting the garbage-can lids and the vehicles, but melting immediately as it hit the street and sidewalks.

A gray-haired dad in ear muffs with three small, well-bundled kids and carrying two sleds came up the block, heading for Prospect Park, as Casey closed the wrought-iron gate behind him, so he backed over to the curb to let them go by while he struggled with the zipper on his jacket. Just as he did so, he heard, felt, or somehow sensed a car door swinging open directly behind him. Then some one or something suddenly grabbed his coat-tail and yanked hard, propelling him into the cavernous back seat of a big sedan.

"What the—?" was as far as he got before everything went black and silent...

✛

It was at least a month and a half, she guessed, since she'd asked Casey for it and he'd given it to her, but she knew it would still be in her purse, because she never threw anything away.

Now, if she could only remember which purse she'd been carrying that night. It would certainly help if she could recall what she was wearing…. It was yellow—the slip of paper—and she'd put Bob's name on it later, she remembered that much, after Casey told her whose phone and address it was, because nothing frustrated her more than anonymous numbers turning up on scraps of paper, when she couldn't for the life of her…and then she'd put it back in the same purse, she was certain of that, but she couldn't remember which purse that was….

No help for it; even trolling slowly through her whole closet hadn't jogged her memory regarding how she'd looked that night on Staten Island. She'd just have to dump them all, one by one, and search through everything.

As it turned out that wasn't too hard—she got lucky on the fourth purse, thanks to Mrrrowski. He'd loved having her dump out those heaps of little things on the closet floor for him to play Gotchya-Mousey! with, and he pounced with special zest on the fourth pile, snatching a canary-yellow Post-It between his paws.

"Mrrrowski! Gimme that!" And there it was, after a brief struggle. But then, naturally, there wasn't an answer to her ring. Bob's message made her smile, though, in spite of her very real distress, and when it was over, after the bullfrog, she said: "Hi, Bob. It's Ru. I'm sorry we—I guess I mean 'I'—haven't seen you in such a long while…"

She'd wanted to, she'd found Bob funny and somehow little-boy sweet, despite his prickly disposition. She'd asked Casey to ask him if he'd care to join them for Thanksgiving, but Bob had replied that, unfortunately, T-day was one of a couple each year when his presence, along with every other living Barrone's, was "de rigeur" on his family's block in the Bronx.

"...I'm calling because Casey seems to have disappeared, the way you did, but apparently from right here on our own street. I know, it sounds crazy, but...I don't know what else to think!"

—C'mon now, she told herself, don't be hysterical—or anyhow, don't let yourself sound that way!

"So if you have any ideas, please call me back." And she left both house and cell numbers. There, that sounded much better....

✢

He returned her call within a matter of minutes. "Tell me about it" was all he said, and then he listened to her fears and anxieties for close to three-quarters of an hour without interrupting once. And after that, he waited nearly half a minute before saying anything himself, to be sure she was really finished. "Tell me again why it must've happened right on your block."

Not 'why you *think* it must've happened...' She liked him for that, too. "Because Casey spoke to our fourth-floor neighbor by the mailboxes, while he was tugging on his coat. She saw him go down the front steps. And he'd just phoned our friend Annette at her store down by Seventh Avenue and asked her if this was a good time to stop by on his way to the subway. I wasn't supposed to know, but Annette always helps him pick out my Christmas present. He's totally shopophobic, poor chump, and that's really the best he can do. But he never got there."

"And this was last night?"

"Yes, and he didn't meet me at BAM as he said he would. And he didn't come home last night. I called the police, and Methodist

Hospital, and everyone else I could think of. That was the first time that's *ever* happened, that he hasn't come home without calling to tell me why."

"You want me to come over?"

"Would you?"

"I'll be right there. Sit tight."

19

Bob showed up quickly, with two very large slices of what he said was and certainly looked like delicious blueberry cheese cake, seven-eighths of which he eventually devoured himself, after multiple urgings for Ru to try it each time he helped himself to another sliver. He listened intently again while she went through everything she knew, surmised or guessed for another hour and a half, but she was disappointed to find that he had very little to offer in terms of things they could *do* about Casey's disappearance—no more than the police at the nearest precinct house, where she'd finally gone at midnight last night, and that was absolutely nothing.

"Come back during business hours in a day or so, when you can file a missing persons report," was all they'd said.

When she ran out of things to say, Bob grabbed the first hint she offered, gave her his cell-phone number, told her to call him if she needed anything or thought of anything else, said good night, and left. She didn't think she could, but she hadn't slept a minute the night before, and as soon as she'd brushed her teeth, stripped and yanked an old night gown over her head, then forced herself to become horizontal, she fell sound asleep and stayed that way until 6:30 A.M., when she opened her eyes to find the cat peering deeply into them, crouched on her chest.

And he stayed close, watching her every move, all through bathroom and breakfast. Ru was sure he must realize that something was terribly wrong, and was offering sympathy....

She decided to go to work because staying home the day before had left her with nothing else to think about but what might have happened, or might still be happening, to Casey. Her work was always demanding, and after an unplanned day off, it was all-engulfing, so she really didn't—because she simply couldn't—give him another thought until she stopped for a Caesar salad and a V-8 at 3:00 P.M. Then the fact hit her like a drop-forge: whenever she went home, there would be no one to greet her but Mrrrowski. He was one hell of a cat, she'd be the first to claim that, but spending the evening with just him again would just make her think of all he lacked as a companion. Tonight what she needed most was a lover...and only Casey could fill that role for her, anymore....

In the end she stayed on in her messy office, straightening up and doing paperwork, until well past eleven.

⁂

Ru woke the next morning—Friday—resolved to do something, she almost didn't care what, to set things in motion. She hadn't heard a word yet from Bob, so that was where she began, by dialing his cell phone. While it was ringing, she looked up at the clock over the refrigerator and discovered that it was only half-past seven, but she let it continue nonetheless. Finally he answered with an indecipherable croak.

"Did I wake you?" she asked, without pity. "It's Ruby. I need to know if you've made any progress."

He made a series of choking and hacking noises, and finally managed to get out: "Depends on what you call progress."

"Well, do you know where he is? Or whether he's dead or alive?"

"Nothing that definite yet, I'm afraid."

"Bob, I'm going nuts here!"

"I'm sorry, Ruby. I'm doing all I—"

"What was the last thing you actually did?"

"The…last thing I…did? You mean to do with finding Casey?"

"Yes, just tell me. Without thinking up the nicest way to put it."

He took her at her word. "Well, I'd picked up some cell phones on Fourteenth Street the other day, you know what I mean, the untraceable kind with time already on them—"

"Yes, I know what you mean. Go on."

"I'd already checked the phone book. There's two numbers for Djokic at that address, one for Boris and another for Dimitri…"

"Go on. What did you do?"

"I tried the Boris number first—twelve rings, no answer. So I tried the other and a woman picked up right away—the daughter-in-law, I figured, there were kids yelling in the background …"

"And?"

"I said…'Hi! I just wondered if you know your father-in-law is going around kidnapping people and chaining them up in your basement?'"

"Good god, Bob!"

"'Who the hell is this?' she yells. 'Just a concerned citizen,' I say, and she hangs up on me."

"You call that 'progress,' do you?"

"Well, I was getting kind of desperate, too, you know? Besides, I'm afraid I was three sheets by that time."

"That does it. I'm going to the police again."

"Sure, why not. They won't do anything besides issuing a missing-person bulletin, which you said they've already done, but who knows, you just might get something going. Anything to stir those Djokics up, at this point. The way I figure it, we've got to get them running scared, somehow, until they show their true colors. Whatever the hell those might be. Sort of like smoking rats out of their holes, is what I guess I mean. Sooner or later, they've got see that they can't get away with whatever it is they're up to...."

Bob was talking to himself by then; Ruby had hung up on him.

20

Detective Metcalf wasn't in yet, but was expected by nine, said a woman who described herself as his partner. Ru decided to be there, waiting, when he got to the precinct house. Since she'd parked the night before on Twelfth Street between Eighth Avenue and the Park, she picked up a croissant and a black coffee at Two Little Red Hens on the way to her car.

It took all of twenty-five minutes to find a parking space, and the nearest one to the police station was seven blocks away, so she fully expected Metcalf to be at his dcsk by the time she got there, but he wasn't. His partner was certainly at hers, though, filling most of the space behind it. Her name was Harriet Thomas, her name plate said, and she was Black, belligerent, and as she herself made clear immediately, "very, very busy." As for Metcalf, it turned out he'd had to go downtown to the courthouse and might be there all day.

"Is that decent coffee you've got in that bag?" Detective Thomas enquired. "You know, Dearie, when you're calling on an officer of the law and expecting them to do something for you, it's customary to bring coffee-and for *them*, too. But you didn't, did you?"

"Of course I did," Ru said with her sweetest smile, offering the bag. "I already had mine, on the way down here." Not true, of course; *choke on it, Dearie!*

The gesture did warm up the air between them by several degrees, and the coffee was excellent, if considerably cooled by now. Detective Thomas didn't care for it too hot, anyhow, especially when it came the way she tried to remember to drink it anymore: without cream or sugar. After a large bite of that truly delicious croissant, she felt vaguely constrained to ask:

"What brings you here?"

Ruby told her, so clearly, succinctly and convincingly that, when Thomas had downed the last crumb and sip, then used three napkins to wipe her hands and face and brush off her desktop, she rose majestically to her feet saying, "How about we take a ride? Wait here, I'll just tell my lieutenant where I'm going."

✠

"Do you have the address with you?" Thomas asked, as they climbed into an unmarked, beat-up, brown sedan. Of course Ruby did, and produced it now from her slender calfskin briefcase. "Mmngh," Thomas grunted, when Ruby read it off to her, "that's *real* Brooklyn, out there. A girl could get lost as all-hell going by the streets, but on the other hand, the BQE must still be bumper-to-bumper at this hour." In the end, she took the streets, starting with Fourth Avenue, and didn't get lost at all, it seemed to Ruby. They made it in under half an hour.

Ru didn't need to see the street sign number to know which house it was—Casey's description was still vivid in her mind. That huge heap of blond bricks may not have been the ugliest thing on Willowbrook Lane, but it probably deserved the ribbon for Most Pretentious. The front door looked as if it belonged on a mausoleum, and was approachable only by a meandering flagstone walkway. Thomas pulled as close to the side entrance as she could, blocking two of the three garage doors.

—Maybe she just doesn't like to walk any further than she has to, Ru decided.

Thomas leaned on the button that activated a set of bells as loud as any cathedral's until the door swung open. She held out her badge like a talisman before her, at arm's length. "You're Mrs. Shannon Djo—Djokic?" she asked. "Are your husband and father-in-law on the premises? I need to speak with them."

"What about?"

"I'll discuss that with them, ma'am. Are they here?"

"Dimmy—my husband—is out on his milk route. I don't know where Mister Djokic is. Maybe he went with him."

—How many young women in this day and age call their fathers-in-law "Mister?" Ruby wondered.

"May we come in?" Thomas said, entering, as Shannon Djokic shrank before her and Ru followed in her wake. They found themselves in a broad hallway between dining room and kitchen. Shannon retreated kitchen-ward, and Thomas went after her. "Is this the way to the basement?" she asked, pointing at a door as they passed it.

"No, that's only a sorta pantry," Shannon said. "I just use it for my good china 'n' silver."

"Where is the basement door, then? We'd just like to take a look down there, if you wouldn't mind." The way that last phrase sounded, nobody in their right mind would ever dare to mind, Ru thought. Who needs a warrant when they have presence like this?

"Uh...sure," Shannon squeaked. "It's that door, right there...."

The detective already had it open and her hand on the light switch. "Thank you," she said, descending, with Ru right behind her.

✛

Considering how new the house was, the basement was a filthy mess. It looked as if the Djokics were in the habit of flinging down whatever they wanted to get rid of from the top of the steps. Thomas stopped at the landing three feet above the floor, stooped, and inspected the rest of the space from there with the aid of a flashlight she produced from her purse.

"See anything?" she asked Ruby, who squatted beside her.

"Shine it over that way again," Ru said. "Look, there's a walled-off section...."

"Yeah, I see it, but how in hell are you going to get to it through all this crap?" Thomas wondered.

"Like this," Ruby told her, taking the flashlight, jumping down and wading over there through god-knows-what. The whole place was rich with foul odors, most of them mildew-related. She was glad she'd worn jeans and a pair of tennis shoes she didn't care about. There was a metal door in the middle of the partition she'd noticed, but it was ajar. She poked in the light, swept it back and forth. "Nothing in here but a furnace, a scrub-sink and a couple of mops," she reported over her shoulder.

"So, you're satisfied?" Thomas asked.

"I guess so," Ru said, reluctantly. There was something she felt, but…nothing she could point to. Something was definitely wrong, she just couldn't think what.

"Then let's get out of here."

Something was wrong in the kitchen, too; Shannon Djokic displayed a degree of relief that was uncalled-for, considering their failure to find anything incriminating. From another room, her children were yelling for her, but she paid no attention.

Back in the car, driving away, Ruby simply said, "Thank you."

"You're welcome," Thomas told her. "Do me a favor, though? If you should have any reason to speak to Detective Metcalf again, don't mention that I brought you out here, okay? He thinks I'm too gullible as it is."

21

Bob Barrone hadn't exactly been idle. An hour after Detective Thomas and Ruby left Sheepshead Bay, it began to snow quite hard, and another hour later, Bob appeared on Willowbrook Lane with a snow-blower. He'd gotten a cousin to introduce him to the local goombah who controlled such activities in the winter and lawn-care in the summer, who wasn't at all averse to Bob replacing the regular guy, as long as he was willing to work for free....

There were barely two inches accumulated, and it was too wet from the warmer sidewalk beneath it to blow very well, but Bob did everything he could to make the job last as long as possible. He wore an old parka with a hood he pulled tight so it showed as little as possible of his face, and he started on the sidewalk opposite the Djokic residence first. The snow-blower masked his limp. He had just switched over to their side when a gray van pulled into their driveway and two men climbed out, clearly the father and son. The side door of the house swung open and a young woman stood in the doorway, yelling something to them—but the trouble with a snow-blower is that it makes one hell of a racket, so Bob couldn't make out a word of what anyone was saying. The woman seemed quite upset, though, and the younger man seemed to be trying to calm her down.

Bob took a chance and choked out the engine on his machine just past the driveway, and knelt down as if he were looking to see what might be wrong with it, just as the woman was saying, "...There was two cops, both women! They wanted to see the basement!"

"So? Did you let them?" the older man wanted to know. "You didn't have to, you know."

"What else could I do?" she wailed.

"Don't worry, it's all right," the younger one said, as the three of them seemed to notice the sudden lack of background racket all at once, and turned to stare in Bob's direction. He took that as a cue to start up the engine again, quickly. As he proceeded along the sidewalk, they went inside and shut the door. When he'd finished the job and was rolling the blower back to where the pickup that came with it sat waiting, he noticed that they'd put the van in the garage, and now there were lights in the apartment above it. Then the side door to the house swung open again, and the younger man yelled, "Hey you! Get the driveway while you're at it, I'll give ya five bucks!"

"It's a lotta driveway," Bob replied. "Make it ten?"

"Seven! There ain't that much snow!"

"No, but it's s'posed to freeze hard tonight! Low twenties, I heard on the radio!" Bob lied.

"Eight! That's my last offer! Knock on the door when you're done!"

The triple driveway was huge, and it took Bob a while to figure out how to do it so that he was always throwing the snow in the right direction, but while he worked, most of his attention was focused on the house, back yard, and garage, searching for places of ingress and egress, as well as areas beyond where the lights shone, where a guy could be unobtrusive.

All in all, it took him more than half an hour, and the son, Dimitri, was back out with greenbacks in hand before Bob had finished his last row.

"Took ya long enough."

"Whadda you care? You ain't payin' by the hour."

The light was very bright by the door where he stood, and Bob's limp was necessarily revealed as he went there for his pay, but Dimitri barely looked at him as he forked the dollars over.

✢

Ruby treated herself to brunch at Dizzy's when she got back to the Slope. She didn't feel she deserved it, but she was famished. As she cornered the remainder of her egg-white omelet with her final toast-crust, she wondered despondently: *What now*? If Casey wasn't in the Djokic's basement, where could he be? *In another basement, you dope*! Or....

There was something Bob had said that she almost but not quite remembered. She got out her cell and dialed his; it switched her at once to message: "Bob—it's Ruby. Please call me at your earliest opportunity." And then she left the same message on his house phone.

Mrrrowski greeted her when she unlocked the apartment door as if she'd been gone for a century. The smells on her tennis shoes and the lower legs of her jeans especially intrigued him. She shucked everything on her way into the bathroom, stuffed it into the washing machine, and took a long shower, as hot as she could stand it.

She was much less interesting to the cat when she came out. Maybe he could sense that she was thinking about returning to her office, just to be as far away as she could get from Casey's absence....

Or maybe not—maybe she'd go swimming; the "Y" schedule magneted to the refrigerator door said there was an adult session in half an hour, just enough time to get her suit on, bundle up against the growing cold, and get down to Ninth Street and Sixth Avenue....

She did forty-eight laps, twice her usual number, and came out of the locker room limp and starving again. There were three messages on her cell, all from Bob. He answered first ring.

"Can you come to the Slope?" she asked, without prelude.

"Can I? I'm almost there already," he said, "Just approaching the Tenth Street exit on the BQE."

"Great. Do you eat Mexican?"

"I eat anything that doesn't eat me first."

"There's a nice little place on the east side of Fifth Avenue, between Tenth and Eleventh...or is it Eleventh and Twelfth?"

"No matter, I'll find it! Ten minutes at most!" He sounded thrilled and forgiven. "I got stuff to tell you, too!"

22

The cheese-and-chicken enchiladas were delicious, Ruby knew, but according to Bob, who scrutinized a neighbor's remaining one of a pair on an adjacent table, they were rather small. After due deliberation, he also ordered two tacos and two empanadas to fill the rest of his empty space: snow-blowing was hard work!

While they were waiting for their food, he told Ru what he'd been up to, and how he'd learned about two female cops having come to the Djokics' to search the basement.

"That was me," she said. "I mean, I was with the one real cop, and mistaken for another, I suppose."

"So you got inside their basement?"

"Yes, and that's definitely not where they've got Casey. Or where they had you, either."

"How do you know?"

"What did it smell like, where you were? Mildew? Was it damp?"

"No to both. It was dry and dusty."

"And that pillar you were chained to—would you please describe it for me again?"

"Cement. Kind of rough. About two—or maybe even three—feet square."

"In other words, it could've been a chimney. And you could've been in their attic."

"Huh! I guess so, yeah."

"Shit! I wish I'd questioned you more closely the first time you told me about it. I'll never get Harriet Thomas to go back there again..."

At which point Bob's tacos arrived. The rest of their order would take longer. "Here, have one of these while we're waiting," Bob offered, and then, through a mouthful, "How's about if I came with you? I could tell her what I know about where they kept me."

The taco was great, she supposed—she'd never been keen on hors d'oeuvres, and that's what a taco was, in her book; much better to save your appetite for the main course, she'd always felt. "…I guess so—we have to try whatever we can…."

It was a quarter past five o'clock by this time, but Thomas was still at her desk. "You again?" was all she said, when she heard who was calling.

"Please, Harriet, would you give me just five minutes of your time? I have some new information." Well, the information may not have been new, but the inferences she was now drawing from it were.

"I'm going to be here past seven as it is with this idiotic paperwork, so five is literally all you're going to get."

"Harriet, you're an angel! We'll be there in fifteen minutes." Actually, it would be at least half an hour, but that shouldn't matter if Thomas was going to be there past seven, anyhow…

"What do you mean, 'we'?"

"I'm bringing a witness!"

⁂

Detective Thomas was less than impressed with Ruby's "witness" when she learned his name and address.

"I've worked the Bronx," she told him, "and I guess I've met most of your family. How's old Antonio? Still racing pigeons? And still as crooked as ever?"

"Look, he may be my uncle, but all I've ever done for him is drive him around in one of his cars," Bob said. "Here's my chauffeur's license, and go right ahead, look for my record—you'll find out I don't have one."

"Uh-huh. That could be because we haven't quite caught up to all of you Barrones yet."

"It could be, but it isn't. I'm no crook, my dad wasn't one either. I'm an anarchist, like he was."

"That's better than a crook?"

"Damn right it is. I've got principles!"

"Well, bully for you. And what have you got to tell me about Ruby's missing boyfriend—"

"Husband!" Ru interjected.

"Okay, missing husband, and the Djo—whatevers?"

"They kidnapped me, too. Six weeks ago. Kept me blindfolded for a week, chained to a cement column that Ruby thinks was a chimney, fed me nothing but stale pizza...."

"That's an interesting story. Any notion why they might've done all that? And most important, where's your proof?"

"...I guess you'll have to take my word for it."

"Delicious. Even if *I* did, there's not a single judge in New York City who would. Speaking of delicious, Ruby, where's my coffee-and this time?"

"I'll go out right now and get you whatever you want."

"Don't bother. It won't earn you another ride to Sheepshead Bay."

"My whole family will swear I disappeared for that week," Bob told her.

"*Your* 'whole family'? 'Disappear' is what you both had better do—right now!"

23

His head was as big as Carnegie Hall. But with all the lights out. He was sitting down, on something slightly springy, and he couldn't move. It took him what seemed like hours to figure out why: his hands were fastened to each other behind his back, around something big, rough, cold, unyielding and square-cornered. That rang a distant bell....

He couldn't manage a sound, either, because his mouth was tightly covered with the same sort of sticky, gauzy stuff that was making it impossible to open his eyes. Only his nose was free; he could make a kind of humming noise through that, but not very loud, and apparently to no effect. His tongue was as dry as a salted herring....

More bells there, but all muffled. Not just where he was, but how and why remained unclear. Only a ready-to-burst bladder kept him from falling unconscious again....

Finally, some degree of focus, and history:

He'd been standing in front of a four-story red brick building with the gold numbers 6-0-0 painted on the arched window above the green front door. 600 Tenth Street! That was where he lived, in apartment 1-R, happily ever after with...Ruby!...Ruby née Schneider, Schneider still for professional purposes, but now and forever Ruby Jones, too.... And there he stood, on the outer edge of the sidewalk, nighttime, a light snow drifting down, and suddenly— he was falling backwards, and then he was here...but where was here?

Bob—Robert S. Barrone: all that had happened to him, too, not very long ago. Here, then, was probably Sheepshead Bay...the Djokics—those sons-of-bitches who'd hit him and left him, in that van....

And why the hell? What did they want from him? He didn't

know, and for the moment, didn't really care. All this remembering was such hard work...forget the bladder, forget everything else, but Ru...he felt himself sliding back again, down to wherever he'd just been....

✦

Up and out again, abruptly, as if from the bottom of a deep well, but everything still just as black. Hands hooked in his armpits, hauling him up. Other hands forcing him forward, with his own hands still behind him, but tight together now, wrapped securely with cold chain....

Limping and stumbling, but not allowed to fall...through a doorway, it felt like, bumped hard against one side, then the other... fingers pulling his coat back, off his shoulders, other fingers undoing his belt, yanking down his trousers and shorts—spun around now, forced downward, onto what could only be a toilet, not very clean, by the smell—and then his hands dragged apart, and the left one yanked upward, fastened somewhere above his head, as far up as it would reach...and a nasal male voice close against his tightly bound ear: "You know what to do! Don't waste any time about it, either!"

Then nothing. Was he alone? He hadn't heard a door close...his right hand went up to whatever that was over his eyes—and *ouch*! Something hard-edged across his knuckles, then the voice again: "Cut that out and do what you're here for, or you'll be sorry!"

Simultaneously, his bladder exploded. Christ, what a relief! Then some one or something shoving a wad of something soft into his free hand.

"Hang on to that, and hurry the hell up!"

As if on command, his bowels let go next.

"Okay, wipe yerself! Quick!"

He did as he was told, as well as he could, then that hand was jerked up, as the other was freed from above, and they were bound together behind him, as before, as he was hauled to his feet, dragged forward, kept upright by those other hands now, under his arms, and the faint sound of water flushing back there. Then pushed down, against the pillar again, his left arm hoisted and fastened to something overhead.

"Sit up straight, goddamn you!"

Something shoved into his free hand, while somebody else unwrapped the bottom half of his face, the sticky gauze tearing at his beard as it came off. When it was gone, and he was enjoying the ability to move his jaw again and open his lips, that same somebody said in his ear, "Eat it! Quick! And don't make a noise above a fuckin' whisper, if you wanna ever eat or drink again, or piss or shit anywhere but in yer pants!"

He knew what it would be before it reached his mouth: stale pizza. But he was ravenous, and gulped it down, as fast as he could chew. The same with the big plastic cup of lukewarm, metallic-tasting water that he was handed next.

"Okay, if you want that gag to stay off, remember what I told ya. There'll always be one of us right here—one peep out of ya, and that gag goes back on, for keeps!"

His ears were still covered by the same gauze that kept his eyelids shut, so he couldn't be sure if the silence that followed in his head was real, or merely due to the fact that he couldn't hear anything that wasn't immediately beside him. In any case, he hadn't heard footsteps receding, a door closing, or any other proof of their departure. After counting to a thousand slowly, twice, he tried a whisper:

"Hello? Are you still there?"

No "Shut up!" Nothing. He repeated himself, a bit louder. Still nothing. Finally, a normal speaking tone. And no reprisal. But he couldn't be sure that any noise he made that might be loud enough to be heard by some one else, some one not a party to his captivity, wouldn't be heard by one of them as well. He couldn't be sure of anything—and that, of course, was the whole point of depriving him of his senses. For how long?

They'd kept Bob for just six days; or anyhow, that was how long they'd had him—had they meant for him to be discovered in the trunk of that old Pontiac? Or to kick his way to freedom? Or had he simply been stashed there temporarily, for some unknowable reason, and they'd intended to retrieve him at some point and continue his torture indefinitely?

There was no telling; and therefore, no indications in Bob's experience of what Casey's future might be. So he had better be prepared for anything....

24

...Funny what happens when you're deprived of your eyes long enough: your brain starts making movies from your memory...whatever you start to think about, there it is, in living Technicolor....

A minute ago he'd been thinking of Ru again, the first time he met her, and migod, there she was, in every luminous detail....

He was in Delhi—no, not India, just the little village on the western edge of the Catskills, in what they call Upstate New York, where the natives all pronounce it *Del' -high*. He'd been staying with friends there, working on yet another unfinishable book project, and she'd come up on the bus that afternoon to help look after the young children of a friend who was in the hospital, and her friend, and the friend's husband, were good friends and neighbors of *his* friends.... And there he was, basking on the porch steps for an afternoon roll-your-own (yes, he still smoked tobacco then, and drank alcohol, too, though not officially, just sneaking enough for a buzz in once in a while) when she came up the walk with her knapsack, looking for her friend's husband, or maybe they'd left keys for her here, but Casey didn't know anything about that....

She needed to buy something for the kids' and her dinner, she was sure of that much, and he offered to walk with her to the Great American (that was the supermarket in the middle of the village), because he walked his friends' dog every afternoon about this time, anyhow. So he put her knapsack inside the door and grabbed the leash off its hook, at which signal Rufus, the over-weight Redbone, always leaped off the sofa and came running. They didn't talk much, just exchanging who they were in the simplest terms possible, why each was in Delhi, and how hot it was that summer, would they ever get any rain, the poor Delaware River was down to nothing but a string of mud holes....

As he followed her up and down the cool, otherwise deserted aisles, pushing her cart for her, he had his first leisurely look at this woman, and liked what he saw, very much, but it certainly wasn't love at first sight; he hadn't realized back then, or for quite a while past that afternoon, that she would become the Great Love of His Life....

And what did he see? Mediterranean beauty, features and body that could have belonged to a classic Greek statue. Wearing sandals, a light cotton skirt, bra-less with a tank top for the country and the weather, smooth olive skin and thick, medium-length black hair, a thoughtfully erect carriage, a mind that seemed to approach every aspect of living with complete seriousness, and a smile that, when he'd earned it, set *his* mind afire.... But he really won his first battle for her heart without even meaning to, by offering to carry her groceries. Later she told him that.

"Shucks, ma'am, that's just the way I was raised," he'd said then, to make her laugh.

✠

Casey continued to remember that torrid summer when they'd grown to like, to begin to know, and gradually to love each other. Weekend trips down to the City on his part, others back up to Delhi on hers. By bus, necessarily, until she bought an old but sound little Ford from her friend's husband and determinedly learned how to drive, at the age of thirty-nine. Without any help from Casey—she knew better than that, she said, and he recognized the wisdom in that decision. He never drove down to Brooklyn himself, because he was not about to subject his venerable—now late-lamented—Chevrolet pickup to the perils of those streets. At most he would take Route 28 to New Paltz, and from thence over the Lordly Hudson, as Paul Goodman called it, to Poughkeepsie, where he'd catch the Metro North train to Grand Central Station, then the #2 Lexington Line subway to Grand Army Plaza. He hated to drive in cities, anyway— state and county two-lane macadam, and gravel and dirt tracks, all across the continent, were always more his speed....

They made sweaty love on her double-bed mattress on the dusty parlor floor of an unreconstructed hundred-year-old brick townhouse in Park Slope, Brooklyn. Sweaty—but majestic from the onset and growing steadily more all-absorbing until it was actually scary, to both of them, each time they launched themselves again on a flight that always took them even deeper into unknown territory....

And they made less sweaty, but just as terrific, love on the fold-out, sagging springs of an ancient "convertible" sofa in the garret at Casey's friends' hundred-and-forty-year-old clapboard house on one of Delhi's handful of quiet, tree-shaded back streets, until he was sure the joyous noise they sometimes made would wake the whole town…and soon that love-making was what they both lived for, all through the week.

Then autumn came, and he gave up the pretence of working on that book, returned to the City, and took up his other life again as itinerant carpenter, plasterer, painter, and jack of all homely trades. There was no reason now for them not to try living together, she said, but he thought *he* knew better this time: Certainly, not where and how she was currently living, where the sink was always full of dirty dishes and everything else full of dirty laundry. Amazing, he thought, how great she always looked in her person, while her home was a dusty shambles….

But living together—being together—was what was needed, what had to come next. So they started looking. He was not about to harness himself to a stiff yuppie-hutch rent and full-time carpentry, he said. But it had to be big enough, they both agreed. A fellow Ruby knew slightly told them about the first-floor Tenth Street apartment coming open: renovated somewhat by the owner, but still your basic shotgun and basically reasonable, four rooms straight through, one after the other, the only hallway the central one with the staircase that you shared with all the other tenants, with one entrance to the front room and another to the kitchen at the rear of the building.

Ruby was sure it was too small, it wouldn't work, Casey said it could, with a few adjustments, beginning with a wall that was clothes cupboards on one side with a narrow door beside them to create two separate spaces, back and front. Now they could get away from each other when they wanted to. Before that, you could literally roll a bowling ball from one end of the apartment to the other….

It worked. After ten years, it was still working. Thanks to friendship with Annette Englander's husband, Phil, who had a cabinetry shop around the corner on Eleventh, Casey became a known neighborhood character, with all the work he wanted within walking distance, and Ruby's office was just on the other side of Prospect Park—a difficult place to get to by subway or bus (it required two transfers on either), but only ten minutes by car, and she could usually find parking within a few blocks at both ends. The rent kept climbing, as rents almost always will, but much more moderately than in most of the Slope, because the building was "Stabilized." Most people they knew were now paying twice as much....

25

—*What if this is some kind of crazy experiment, to see how long a human being can last under such conditions, before going totally nuts—or before it turns that person into a kind of moral silly putty that can then be induced to take any shape, commit any act you tell him to?*

Judging as best he could—from the number of times he'd been fed and taken to the toilet—he'd been wherever he was for three days now, and he was beginning to learn what he had to do if he was going to have any real chance of surviving and perhaps eventually escaping this experience.

Reliving early days with Ruby was fine, it could well be the key to his survival, if he could stay focused on the wonder of what they had, and avoid pitying himself for presently being deprived of it.

Yesterday he'd started exercising his legs as well as he could, in his situation. Fifty leg-lifts to begin with, at the hip and then at the knee, and fifty ankle flexes, back, forward, left, right. Tomorrow he'd raise the figure by ten, and so on until he was at one hundred. And bicycling as fast as he could in the air while he counted slowly to ten thousand (he'd only managed seven hundred just now).

The effort would make him even hungrier than he was already, on two slices of pizza a day, but that couldn't be helped—otherwise his legs, the left one especially, would stiffen up on him until he couldn't even walk, let alone run, should an opportunity ever arise....

☩

Another thing about being deprived of his eyes and ears was the increasing difficulty he found in discerning the difference between consciousness and sleep. The only times he knew for sure now that he was awake was when he was exercising or else being marched to the toilet, then fed and given his daily ten or twelve ounces of water....

He knew he had to somehow persuade his captors to communicate with him. It was his only chance of learning anything about his situation. He did what little he could to appear compliant, long-suffering, uncomplaining, and he spent hours considering what he could say that might be rewarded with a response. All to very little purpose, because his windows of opportunity were so short, and always without notice.

"Please, won't you tell me what you want from—"

"Shut up and eat that, or I'll take it away!"

"...I just want to know what I—"

"Goddamn you! I said shut up!"

"Isn't there anything I can—"

"NO! Now *shut up!*"

✠

...If I ever tried to write about this experience—just supposing I ever get the chance—I know the perfect title for it, but it's already been used, and used perfectly: *Hope In The Dark*, by an extraordinary writer named Rebecca Solnit. But I'd be meaning it in a very different way from the way she did. My way would be literal: here I sit, in the dark, but I keep hoping. Even if I'm not always hopeful, I'd forget all the times I wasn't, I'm sure, if I ever did manage somehow to get out of this predicament alive. I think anybody would—and we'd focus on the times when we *were* genuinely hopeful.

Anyway, Solnit used it for a collection of essays meant to look back over the last decade or so and point out all the real but mostly unknown reasons for actual hope in these desperate, scary years. In building an argument that the outcome is not necessarily going to be Them, everything, Us, total defeat, she never denies the reality of that desperation, that scariness. "The future is always dark" is a point she makes again and again, and "history is like weather" in that it never ends: "defeats are permanent, victories temporary," and that's also why "it's always too soon to go home"—home from the struggle to save the world, that is, the struggle that never ends because the world will always need saving, from us, meaning the species, for as long as we-the-species hangs around....

I went home in that sense a long time ago, Casey had to admit: "burned out," I called it, sick to death of meetings that everyone there was trying to subvert, divert and convert, instead of trying to contribute to the general grasp of the problem and to reach some practical, positive consensus. So I tuned in and dropped out (having already turned on a long time before then), and took my family off to the Rocky Mountains to wait out Armageddon, which we all believed was well on its way: hadn't we moved onto our land the weekend of Kent State? If anyone could have told us of Watergate, only a couple years away, we would have been absolutely certain it would all come crashing down. But we were so naïve—we never realized how elastic, how devious and inscrutable, the State could be....

26

By the fifth day, he found he was losing track. Hadn't it been longer than that by now, surely? He needed to keep count on something—and his fingers were out, he was barely aware of their existence, back there behind the pillar. He only knew for sure he still had them when he was holding a slice of pizza to his mouth, or the water cup. Whenever he thought of it, he forced himself to move and count all ten digits, repeatedly, and that helped quite a bit; but best of all for keeping track of things, he decided, were his toes—he couldn't see them any more than he could see his fingers, but they *were* in front of him, and he could imagine them out there at the end of his legs, in those must-be-reeking socks and boots that hadn't been off his feet all this while. He could wiggle each one, individually, and even talk to them.

—When they start talking back, he told himself, I'll know I've been in here too long....

He was captured on a Tuesday night, that much was clear in his mind, so Day Number One was his left little toe—Wednesday—and today was the left big toe—Sunday—and tomorrow would be right big toe, AKA Monday....

"So...day after tomorrow would be right second toe, also the end of Week Number One...."

In some ways it helped, knowing this, in others it didn't. In a way, it was orienting, because now he could figure out the date: today had to be the twelfth of December, so Christmas/Xmas was only thirteen more days away, in other words two weeks from yesterday. So C/X would fall on a Saturday this year....

But on the other hand: if he'd already been gone five days, was *anything* being done, by *anyone*, to get him out of here? He considered the problem again from the other side, when it was Bob Barrone who had disappeared, and how hard it was to make the police take what he'd told them seriously.

How is Ruby taking it, my absence, I mean? God, how I hate to hurt her, even when I can't help it! Who would she turn to, for help? Do we know anybody to call at a time like this? Some one who's used to dealing with kidnappings and hostage situations—I don't think there's anyone like that, in either of our address books....

✢

Soon after his pizza and water, he found, was the best time to do his exercises. If he waited until he'd slept it was too hard to know how long he'd been asleep, hence how much time was left before toilet, pizza, and water would happen to him again. It was also when he had the most energy. Then, while his endorphins were still dancing, he would return to his meditation on his life with Ruby....

It hadn't all been as easy, or as smooth, as it seemed to him now. Once they'd begun living together, two other portentous subjects loomed between them: marriage, and children. He'd been there, both places, she hadn't. She'd been fast approaching forty, he was fourteen years older, and his sons were grown men with lives of their own.

Actually, both subjects had been raised much earlier, by Ruby, soon after they'd met, in fact, and he hadn't exactly said no to either—good god, he didn't want to say no to anything she wanted from him, ever, if he could possibly help it. And that, of course, was the problem....

Marriage was one thing, and pretty easy, really. He didn't believe he was cut out for it, and he didn't think that governments or anything else had any business in whatever two grown, sane people decided between themselves, but if that piece of paper would make Ru, and her family, any happier or more cordially inclined to him, then, what the hell, why not?

And when he learned, early on, that her parents had retired from the Bronx to Las Vegas, Nevada—well, sure, that sounded like the perfect place to do something he'd sworn he'd never, ever do again. So fly out over a long weekend, meet the folks, go to one of those tacky little chapels with the quarter-hour ceremony and the video they sell you afterwards, fly back with the license in her suitcase, nothing to it, right?

That left the matter of Children, with a capital C—and given her age, she felt it had to be very soon or never. So he considered it—as seriously as he'd ever considered anything, including why he had ever come into existence, and the more he thought about it, the more he remembered what was actually involved, and the less capable he knew he was, of doing and being all that again (if he'd ever been). He'd be nearly seventy before the kid, or kids, left high school. He recalled only too clearly what those teen years could be like—and he'd be…no. He couldn't do it again, that's all, and as much as it terrified him to tell her so, straight out, he knew that was exactly what he had to do.

—What if she decided that becoming a mother was more important to her than he was? Well, that'd be a tough one, bud, wouldn't it?

The most insidious temptation was to say nothing, and gamble that one or the other of them would prove physically incapable. Just because his sperm was viable in his early twenties didn't mean it still was, three decades later, after everything that he'd done or been exposed to—I said NO! god damn it, that's no way to be, definitely not when it's the woman with whom I want to spend the rest of my life….

So he told her; and trembled, while he waited to learn what her reply would be. And of course it wasn't as clear or simple as his memories would like to make it. One telling is never enough for something that momentous: he had to say it again and again before she accepted that, on this one question, his mind could never be made to see it her way. And even all these years after time itself had made the matter moot, happenstance or an incautious word could pitch them both back there, where the hurt still lurked.

He was even more convinced now that he had been right, that if they had attempted to produce and raise children, they (or come on now, let's be honest: *he*) would never have made it, and that she'd be raising them alone now, or with someone better able to share the responsibility, and he'd be off on his own, god-knows-where. But there was no sense in trying to tell Ru that—or ever to broach the subject again….

27

Five days, Ruby told herself. *Casey's been gone five whole days already, and just what in hell am I doing about it? Nothing!*

And what could she do? She couldn't think of anything that might help. She'd phoned the precinct again but she hadn't been able to speak to anyone besides the desk sergeant. Metcalf and Thomas were both "too busy." When she asked what sort of actions would have followed the issuance of the MP bulletin, she was told it had been faxed to every precinct in the City.

"And what did they do with it?"

"Do? They filed it."

"And that's that?"

"Yeah, pretty much. Unless there are further developments."

"Such as?"

"He turns up somewhere."

"Great."

"Look, what did you expect? A door-to-door, borough-wide manhunt?"

"At least."

"Well, you go find us the funding, and we'll happily do that for everyone who goes missing."

She called Bill di Marco, Casey's lawyer, to ask if he had any helpful suggestions. Sympathy he had plenty of, but skepticism, too. To begin with, he found it extremely hard to believe Casey's disappearance could have anything to do with the Djokics.

"What do you know about them?" she asked.

"Very little, to be truthful. Nothing beyond what we got in that deposition, really."

"Then how do you know what they're capable of doing?"

"Well, I guess I don't, but it just seems extremely unlikely."

"So does his disappearance."

"I suppose you're right."

"How would I go about finding out anything more about those people?"

"Well, private investigators are very expensive, and you don't want—"

"Can you give me the name of one you trust?"

"Well, sure, but like I said—"

"Who is it?"

"Henry Neville and Associates—"

"Got the number handy? … Thanks, bye "

⸸

Henry himself answered the phone. When told what she wanted, he said he required a three-hundred-dollar retainer for routine background checks. There was no telling how much more it might cost, until it was done. The investigation would begin once a check for that amount was received, deposited, and cleared.

"Where are you? I'll bring you three hundred right now, in cash."

"Very good. Then I—we will begin this very afternoon."

That was Day Four. This morning, Henry had called back and told her to please come by and pick up her retainer.

"Why, what's wrong?"

"I can't help you."

"And you won't tell me why?"

"Let's just leave it that I was advised, by someone whose advice I take very seriously, to decline to assist you in this matter. I'm sorry."

"I wish you were sorry enough to explain your decision."

"…Look, these simply aren't people you want to mess around

with, okay? That's really all I can tell you."

"Then just send me a check for the three hundred."

"Will do. Right now. Goodbye."

When Ruby relayed this exchange to Bob Barrone, he said, "I'm not too surprised." Why not, she wondered. "Because these creeps are in bed with the government somehow. My uncle admitted that much."

"Well, gee, thanks for not telling me until now."

"Sorry. I thought I had. But I guess it was just Casey I told... look, let me see what I can accomplish here. *Please*, Ruby. I think I know somebody who's not so scared of a G-man or two...."

28

Bob didn't call her back until ten of eleven the next night, minutes after she had made up her mind to call him again, if he hadn't done so before the hour was up.

"Hi!" he said. "Sorry it's so late, but I've been having my ear chewed on all evening. I got a real education. Boy, I should've thought of this guy right off, what he don't know or can't find out is...well, there can't be much he doesn't or couldn't, if you follow. Confidentially, he's another cousin of mine, but on my mother's side. Totally different sort of family there—"

"I'm sure your whole genealogy is absolutely spellbinding, Bob, but what matters to me right now is what you learned about the Djokics, and how it can help us find Casey."

"Well, you tell me: to begin with, Old Man Djokic—actually, he's a couple years younger than I am—is a Crote."

"Crote? Do you perhaps mean Croat, or Croatian?"

"All I know is when Bobby says it, it sounds like Crote. Shit, wouldn't you know, there I go—"

"Revealing your source?"

"Right. I might as well tell you. You don't know his last name, anyhow. Bobby was named after me. He's a total nut on what he calls Bee Cee—The Balkan Conflict. He told me about it for hours, how there's these three sorts of people that've all been living right on top of each other for all kinds of generations, I mean like *hundreds*, and they hate each other worse than Jews and Arabs do, worse than Brits and Irish, so they're always picking on each other whenever they can—but you and me, we couldn't tell them apart, not even if we were looking at them naked, except that the circumcised ones are most probably Muslins, AKA Albanians—"

"Muslims."

"In my family we say it either way. Don't matter—we all know what we're talking about."

"Fair enough. So there's Muslims, AKA Albanians, or Bosnians, who ran the governments in that part of the world for the Turks when they owned the area a few centuries back, and there's Serbs, who if they aren't atheistic communists, they're Greek or Russian Orthodox, and then there's Croatians, who are Roman Catholics and used to be the Nazis' finest concentration camp guards."

"I guess you've heard this story before."

"Yes indeed. Tell me, Bob, just a hunch—how old is Bobby?"

"Thirteen. It was his first war. Nowadays all he can talk about, unless you say 'Bee Cee' quick, before he gets going, is Iraq and

Afghanistan. Or Lebanon and Syria. Or, if he's really depressed, Israel and Palestine."

"And how did Bobby find out for us that Djokic is a Croat?"

"Turns out the guy's famous. I mean, he's in books. At least he's famous if you're a Bee Cee nut, like Bobby."

"Why's he in books?—Wait, I'm afraid I can guess—"

"Yeah. Because he's a monster. If you're a Serb or an Bosnian, he is, anyhow. They call him the Arch-Demon of a place I can't pronounce."

"That part of the world is full of places pronounceable only by them. And if you dig back far enough, there were atrocities by one side or another in all of them. What else does Bobby know about him?"

"Well, he looked him up on his computer. Bobby's—well, he's pretty sharp with that damn thing. I mean, he gets into all kinds of files: banks', corporations', the Pentagon's—he's been doing that kind of stuff since he was eight. Ivan Djokic, turns out he's over here as 'a guest of the nation.' But his son's a citizen—his mom was an American. She left Ivan, and Croatia, in the late 'eighties, brought little Dimmy back to Brooklyn. She died of some kind of cancer in the late 'nineties...."

"How so, 'a guest of the nation'?"

"I asked that, too. Turns out that's a direct quote from what Bobby found in the Pentagon records. He said it literally means Ivan's over here in the hands of You Ess Army Military Intelligence. That old oxymoron. Bobby thinks he's here because if he was over there, the Serbs or the tribunal in The Hague would probably have him by now."

"Odd he's still using his own name, then."

"Think so? I don't. I think it tells you a lot about what kind of guy he is, though. I've got a bunch of relatives who feel the same way about our surname: You live and die a Barrone. You don't go sneaking around underneath any alias. I'll bet Ivan's proud as hell of everything he's done, and thumbing his nose at the Serbs."

"But he's understandably anxious to keep his name out of official court records. So his son says *he* was driving."

"Dead right. Dimitri, by the way, didn't have a pot to piss in until Ivan showed up a few years back, bought that little delivery business and made his son a full partner, bought that house, too, but put everything in the son's or Shannon's name, just to be on the safe side."

"What else did Bobby turn up?"

"...I think that's about it."

"Nothing about what Ivan and Dimitri might be up to these days, in Brooklyn, besides delivering milk?"

"I'm afraid not."

"A man like that does not come to America to contentedly spend the rest of his life delivering milk."

"I'd have to agree with you there. So it seems he's taken up the hobby of kidnapping people."

"Just for something more interesting to do?"

"Who knows, and who really cares? All we've got to find out for sure is where they've got Casey—*is* he in their attic, like you think?—and how the hell to get him back...."

29

Wherever he was, it was unheated, but it hadn't—at least so far—grown colder than the upper forties, he guessed, so even with his jacket as it was, unzipped and spread wide, he hadn't really suffered yet from being cold...but right now it must be as chilly as it's ever gotten since he'd been here, probably low forties if not upper thirties, so his guess was it must be late night now, or early morning...and let's see, it's Day Number Ten, soon to become Eleven if it's not already, so it's late Friday or early Saturday, the Seventeenth or Eighteenth of December....

He wondered what Ru was doing just then. He pictured her asleep in the middle of their king-sized futon—though she firmly denied it, she always took over the middle whenever she had it all to herself. He imagined her snoring softly, in spite of her certainty that she never did such a thing. And Mrrrowski, of course, would be right up there with her, probably curled in a ball on top of Casey's pillow....

—Christ, Jones, what do you think you're doing? You just made yourself cry! Don't you know you can't afford those hot tears running down your cheeks? Not on ten or twelve ounces of water a day, you can't! Think about some time back then, when you were there, too, and part of it, not about now: now, for the time being, is just something to get away from, one way or another!

✣

It was still dark when Ru woke that morning, only an hour or so after Casey had finally fallen back asleep. She turned on the light to read the alarm clock: five-twenty-two....

She tried rolling over, reshaping her pillow, tucking the sheet carefully around her shoulders, but it was no use. Twenty minutes later she flung the covers back, to Mrrowski's intense displeasure, pulled on her robe and slippers, and went out to the kitchen to make herself a tall cup of chai with honey and a couple spoonfuls of milk. She sat at the round oak table to drink it, thinking miserable thoughts. It seemed, at that hour, as if all she had accomplished since Casey's disappearance was to fall irretrievably far behind in her work. And that wouldn't do, it wouldn't do at all. She wrote grants for a living, for nonprofits, mostly of a medical nature since that was her own background, and all her clients had inexorable deadlines to meet, like rent and wages....

—That's not all I'm falling behind in, she told herself, looking around the kitchen and what she could see from there of the bedroom and bath. I've let this apartment become even worse than when Casey was in the hospital! What if his key were to turn in that lock this minute? What would I feel most? Joy at his return, or shame at what a lazy cow I've been?

Well, that, at least, was a problem she could deal with, beginning right now. She stripped off her robe and gown and got into an old pair of pants and one of Casey's work shirts, putting up her hair in a giveaway cap from the paint store that used to be on the corner of Seventh Street and Seventh Avenue. Then she put a load of towels in the washer and pulled the sheets and pillowcases off the bed for load number two—again to the cat's intense discomfiture.

"You'd better get off there, and stay off!" she informed him. "I may have been letting things slide around here, but from this morning onward, kiddo, we're going to live as if Casey's already back home, you hear?"

By nine, when Ru stopped for blueberry-coconut granola, two-percent milk and a sliced banana, she'd scrubbed just about everything that was scrubbable in both the bathroom and the kitchen, she'd remade the bed with sheets and pillow cases straight from the dryer, she'd carried out three loads of garbage and four of newspapers and catalogs, and she'd washed every dirty dish, glass and pot she could find, all through the apartment.

Next, she decided as she downed another chai, she'd dust and vacuum in the front rooms, and hang up all her clothes in the closet that weren't going into the washer or up the block to the Korean cleaners. And then she'd shower and wash her hair, get dressed, and go put in at least eight hours at her office, dropping off the dry-cleaning on her way to her car.

At the sight and sound of such furious activity, Mrrrowski had soon retreated to the back yard, chilly as it was out there.

The car was on Twelfth between Eighth and the Park again, and she'd worked off so many calories, she figured, that she could afford to treat herself to a brioche and a decaf cappuccino from Two Little Red Hens.

They—the municipal They (why didn't their traffic-blockers say "DIG WE MUST" anymore?)—were tearing up big chunks of Prospect Park Southwest again, so she decided to go around by Army Grand Plaza for a change. It was longer, but traffic shouldn't be bad on a Saturday if she avoided the Jamaican neighborhood, where they'd all be out in their cars in the middle of the street, having great conversations with all their neighbors, at, let's see—oh, wow, it's twenty to two already, they'd certainly all be out in the street by this time....

As she made the lights coming around the Central Library and onto Eastern Parkway, a delivery truck pulled out in front of her from a service access at the rear of the building. She was about to move over into the left lane to pass it when she caught a glimpse of what it said on the side panel—the only word she was sure she'd read right was "MILK," but that was enough; she thought she knew who it had to be, and she dropped back behind it, just out of curiosity...better make that three cars behind it, though, she advised herself a moment later, just to be on the safe side....

30

Bob Barrone woke at half-past noon that Saturday, with Barbara Stanwyck scratching peevishly at his wrinkled sheets, and a fresh idea glowing brightly in his mildly hung-over mind (but I should've thought of this *last* Saturday!):

Maybe it's those Doity Djokics' unholy ritual—to hold a victim for a week or so of torturing with the blindfold and pizza-and-water diet, and then on a Saturday night, dump him off somewhere, in something he can work himself out of, eventually, like the Pontiac's trunk. So maybe I ought to check out that neighborhood tonight....

Not, of course, in the Pontiac, which was all Bob had for wheels these days, having been ordered by his Uncle Antonio to turn in his set of family car and garage keys; he'd be told when, if ever, he could have them back. Those Crazy Crotes would be sure to recognize the Pontiac. But he could always trade it for the pickup that came with the snow-blower, since he knew where that was parked and had been cheerfully furnished with all the keys he needed there.

Bob rolled out of bed, landed more or less on his aching feet and legs, and shuffled to the bathroom with his cat forcing herself between and around his ankles. Leaning over the toilet tank, left arm braced against the wall, he considered one of his adult life's eternal questions: to shave or not to shave? One sweep of a palm across his chin told him he had better do it, and since the easiest way to shave was while he was in the shower, he'd do that, too—he couldn't remember the last time he'd taken one, but a cautious sniff at an armpit convinced him it was overdue.

A bath and shave deserved clean clothes, but who knew what he might be getting into, so he pulled on a set of black sweats, top and bottom, over thermal underwear, all out of his dresser, plus a pair of athletic socks, and then laced on his eight-inch waterproof snow boots. A midnight-blue down vest and a black billed cap with earflaps from his front-door closet completed his costume. Then he took his time packing several other things in an old blue gym bag.

A glance into his dismal kitchen persuaded him, as usual, to go out for a diner breakfast. Barbara Stanwyck was still glued to his legs, though, so he reached into the closet for the box and shook some dry food into her bowl, checking to be sure there was plenty of water in the other one. God knows she didn't need his offering, she was damn near obese (the vet said she was that already), but he couldn't resist when she mewled so sweetly....

By the time he'd put himself on the outside of three eggs over-easy, a double order of sausage, rye toast, a short stack of buttermilk pancakes drowned in real maple syrup, and three well sugared and well creamed cups of coffee, he was feeling pretty good, but he decided to pop a couple of oxycodones anyway, for the throbbing and creakiness in his ankles and knees. The highways were pretty clear all the way to Coney Island, but by the time he'd switched vehicles and gotten to Sheepshead Bay, the bleary winter sun was already sinking into the miasma over New Jersey.

There was nothing doing on Willowbrook Lane—too cold outside even for kids, and no snow this weekend to fool around in. He spent an hour creeping through the surrounding streets, by which time it was completely dark, finding nothing much to investigate. He swung past the Djokic house two more times: there were dim lights on in the back and in the apartment over the garage, and a blinking xmas tree visible through curtains on the otherwise dark downstairs front windows, but no other signs of life anywhere. All three garage doors were shut.

Five of the other seven houses on their side of the street had gone hog-wild with xmas decorations, including santas, sleighs and reindeer on the roofs of three of them, but there were none on the Djokic property. The far side of the street was well lighted, too, with plastic angels and snowmen and two rudolphs as well as santas, all except for the house directly opposite the Danovs', which was completely dark, with a four-by-six-foot realtors' sign on the front lawn which simply said "FOR SALE," with the agent's name and phone number.

Decision time: Bob could continue to creep the streets, cover every square yard of Sheepshead Bay looking for possible places where Casey might have been dumped off, or....

He'd copied that realtor's number when he ran the snow-blower, and he'd tried calling it the other day. When he told the receptionist which address he was interested in, she'd said, "Soo-reee! We're no longer showing that property at this ty-ime!"

Which was interesting. What if that was where they were holding Casey, and where they'd kept him—Bob—when they had him? Whoever had crept up and stuck a hypodermic in his arm while he was watching the Djokic house must have come from that side of the road, at his back, or else he would've spotted them.

It was worth checking out. Question was, how to approach it? Straight up the front walk? Not this early in the evening, with all those xmas lights shining on him. It would probably take him five or ten minutes, at least, to figure out and get the best of the locks and alarm systems—that was too long to stand on a front step in full view of, if not the whole curving street, at least three-quarters of it....

Bob explored the next street over; there was a lot of light there, too, but the house he figured must be directly opposite the empty one on Willowbrook sat back on a double lot with a fair amount of trees and shrubbery around it, and what's more, it didn't have many lights on at all: just about the number that people might put on timers if they were spending their holidays elsewhere.

Two blocks still farther away, there was a bar facing a deli, both with mostly empty parking lots. Bob chose the bar's, because they'd be staying open later. He parked in a darkened area toward the back, then dug into the gym bag he'd packed before he left home, and loaded himself with all the stuff he might need:

- a flashlight that clipped to his cap with a cord running down to a switch he slipped on his wrist,
- gloves made of some plastic that was thinner, tougher and more pliant than kidskin,
- a top-of-the-line eight-tools-in-one gadget,
- a webbed belt with hooks and pockets, onto which he clipped the gadget and his next selections,
- an all-purpose knife with an "unbreakable!" folding five-inch blade,
- four figs-and-filberts granola bars,
- a flat pint canteen, full of hundred-proof bourbon,
- a tiny first-aid kit,
- a flat steel pry bar,
- fifty feet of slender nylon cable that would bear twice his weight,
- a super-light pair of binoculars,
- another of infrared glasses,
- a throwing knife, and finally,
- a loaded nine-millimeter Glock in a leather holster and a harness that clamped it beneath his left armpit along with two more full clips.

Bob spent a good deal of his waking time poring through arcane catalogs that sold ingenious and often ingeniously lethal merchandise, most of it lovingly handcrafted. Though money was of no consequence to him if he really wanted something, he dearly loved a good bargain, some doodad beautifully handmade, for less than the big sporting companies charged for the inferior, mass-produced counterpart.

Unlike most of his family, Bob also loved guns and knives. Barrones typically looked at such things much the way an architect would at a shovel or a hammer. They simply weren't raised to be hands-on; they preferred to hire someone to use those crude tools, when their use couldn't be helped, and they looked upon such times as failures, because the best way to get what you want is through finesse, and the making of deals, and you always should come out ahead because, at last resort, you're always—as the man said— willing to make offers that can't be refused.

Bob, on the other hand, dreamed of total independence in a very thinly populated world: on his own in the post-atomic wilderness, or wherever. And always not just fully, but very thoughtfully and handsomely equipped....

He walked back to the street before Willowbrook, slightly thicker through the middle and clinking a bit as he moved. There was no sign of other life anywhere, aside from the blinking colored lights; not a car, not even a dog-walker. As he slipped into the bushes just beyond the house he figured must be opposite the one that claimed it was for sale but wasn't, not a single dog barked....

31

Following the milk truck, Ru was soon in sections of Brooklyn she didn't know at all. The following itself was easy, though. Traffic was light but brisk, the truck's driver seemed to be in no hurry, and staying three or four cars back was not a big problem. Eventually she saw signs for JFK Airport, Coney Island, and the BQE. Then the truck signaled left and turned off into a side street, and from that one into another with a 'No Exit' sign.

Ru stopped where she could see down the dead-end street, and watched the truck disappear backwards into a brick building. Less than five minutes later, a gray van came out and headed toward her. She'd never seen it before, but she'd heard enough about the gray van to know that was what she should follow when it headed back the way they'd come, so she U-turned after a decent interval and soon caught up with it.

In another ten minutes, landmarks were becoming more familiar; she must be approaching Sheepshead Bay from a different angle than when she'd come out here with Harriet Thomas. The next time the van signaled a turn, she recognized Willowbrook Lane and stopped just short of the corner, where the curve in the street allowed her a view of the garage end of the Danovs' house. The van disappeared into it, and she was debating whether to let this gambit go and try to find her way back to her end of Brooklyn, when the van reappeared, heading toward her. She slid down in her seat and watched it turn the corner and drive right past her.

She'd had two good looks at the driver before, early on and then when he came out from the street where he'd left the milk truck, and this definitely wasn't him—he was late twenties, sour-featured, with short dark hair, and she'd assumed he was the son. This guy was twenty at most, more likely still in his teens, in a green tee shirt and purple down vest, with a shaved head, half a dozen rings on his ear and garish blue tats on his bare biceps. And there was another kid beside him, with long dirty-blond hair and a watch cap yanked down over his ears.

Ru was so surprised she nearly missed what was happening back down the street at the Djokics': as soon as the door where the van had reappeared rolled shut, the one beside it opened, and out came a new black Hummer. It followed the van, and as it swung past her, she saw that the son was driving this now, and the man beside him had to be the father.

She let them get nearly two blocks past her before she turned around and followed, grateful that she was driving one of the least conspicuous vehicles that Detroit ever built, a nondescript little blue sedan, some kind of Ford. She'd read or been told a million times what the model was, but the name was so nondescript, too, at least to her ears, that she could never remember it on request, and always had to look at the registration to be sure....

⚜

Soon it was clear that they were headed Long Island-ward, past JFK and onto the Sunrise Highway, past Valley Stream, Freeport, Massapequa, then down to Babylon and onto the Robert Moses Causeway, and from there to Ocean Parkway. Ru was glad she'd filled the tank a few days ago....

In summer there would be bumper-to-bumper traffic out here, but now there were no other cars to hide hers behind, so she was preparing to stop in Oak Beach when she saw they were doing the same thing.

Driving past them, she saw in her rear-view mirror that they were just parking the Hummer, and the two Djokics were piling into the vacated seats at the front of the van. In a few minutes, the van roared past her, and neither Djokic seemed to grant her as much as glimpse.

Several more minutes after that, about halfway to Jones Beach, she passed the van again, now pulled off onto the shoulder, and everyone was piling out of the back but the one she had guessed was the son. There werc six young guys, she saw now, all on the ground, and they all were looking back at her as she approached. So was the father, who had been passing out black duffels from inside the back of the van, but before she was close, he pulled the doors shut in front of his face.

She drove on at the speed limit, with her chin poked over the steering wheel as if she hadn't even noticed them. It felt dumb, but she couldn't think of anything better to do. When she reached the closed-for-the-season gates to Jones Beach, she sat for ten minutes by the clock on her cell phone, and then she drove slowly back the way she'd come. She'd noted the mile-marker, and she was fairly sure she'd spotted the tracks where the van had pulled over. It was gone now, and so were all those men.

Less than half a mile farther on back in the direction of Oak Beach, there was a place to pull off. Curiosity made her do it; but she sat there for another five minutes, thinking about what Casey would do if their roles were reversed, and then briefly about what she might be getting into, before impulsively climbing out, locking the car, climbing over the guard rail, and skidding down the bank to the beach on the ocean side.

32

There was an intimidating eight-foot hurricane fence with razor-wire along the top separating the two back yards, but there was also a door from the back garden at the rear of the garage, with just a padlock on a flimsy hasp—would you believe it?—and sure enough, there was a twenty-foot aluminum extension ladder hanging on an inside wall that Bob could disassemble, and he simply had to lean one half securely against that side of the fence, carry the other with him as he climbed, sling it over on the other side, make sure it was stably situated, swing himself over (the only tense moment, with coiled razor wire inches from his testicles), and then climb down the other half.

He left the ladders as they were for his retreat, and proceeded across a neat but busy back yard with a gazebo and a good deal of expensive shrubbery and perennials, over slippery flagstones to the back door of the house that wasn't for sale.

No indications of a sophisticated alarm system, just a cheap scare-the-kids-away variety, which occupied Bob less than a minute. There was nothing very new in the lock department, either, so he was in the kitchen in just under four minutes from hitting the ground on this side of the fence.

He stood still and silent now for several minutes, getting his bearings, listening for anything at all and deciding he wouldn't need his flashlight much, which was good, because you could never be sure a next-door neighbor wouldn't chance to be looking that way. All the windows had Venetian blinds, but a flashlight beam will usually find its way through those, and through wooden shutters, too....

Bob hadn't been lying when he told Detective Thomas that he was an anarchist, not a criminal, but that didn't mean he hadn't been taught by his uncles the same things his cousins learned, back on the block after school. And they were mostly a lot of fun to learn, unlike just about everything his teachers taught him.

The kitchen was as fully equipped as Bob was, with every mod-con imaginable. He found the door to the basement in two tries.

—Check it out first? Why not?

Down there he had to use the flash, no help for it, but he took it off his cap and used that to shield it from the lightly curtained windows, holding it at knee-level, shining straight down. There was a rec room with a built-in bar, a few unwashed glasses and no liquor; a workout room with a great set of weights and a top-of-the-line exercise bike; a toy, computer and TV room for little kids; and a sort of meditation room, that's what it seemed to be, with rolled mats still hanging on one wall, god's eyes and a bearded guru's portrait on another, a brass bowl half full of the ashy remains of incense cones in the center of the floor.

But there was no sign of Casey, no pillar like the one Bob was sure he'd been chained to, and no entrance to a tunnel running under the street to the Djokics' basement, like Bob had been hoping for, though he wouldn't have admitted it, not even to himself....

He climbed back up the basement stairs and tried all the other doorways from the kitchen, which led him into the unfurnished dining and living rooms, then the grownups' TV room, and something with floor-to-ceiling shelves, a desk and easy chairs he supposed was meant to be a study. Then he returned to the staircase opposite the front door, and slowly mounted that. There were four bedrooms on the second floor, all empty, and two spacious baths. The Mawster Bawth, as Bob pronounced it in his head, even had a bidet, surely a rare fixture in Sheepshead Bay.

The attic door was locked, which raised his hopes, but it only took a skeleton key and less than ten seconds to get open. The third step up creaked loudly—was that a natural alarm? Bob froze in place with his right hand on his unsnapped holster, waiting to find out what would happen....

✠

Somehow Ru knew it would be the ocean side; and if it wasn't, she'd simply climb over the road when she decide to call it quits over here, and walk back on the sound side....

The wind was stiff and steady, out of the southeast, with a fine salt spray, and she was glad she'd had her yellow windbreaker with her on the back seat of her car, and her blue beret, which she could and did pull down over her ears. Gloves would've been nice, too, but you couldn't always have everything, and she wanted to keep her hands inside her pockets, anyhow. The tide was just going out, and she didn't spot any tracks on the smooth, wet beach, only a few old ones above the high-tide mark. There wasn't much debris, either, only the occasional well-rounded piece of wood, most of them so water-worn you couldn't tell if they were formerly lumber or pieces of trees, and Paleolithic-looking horseshoe crab shells.

She spotted him long before he saw her, but there was nowhere to hide, and scrambling back up to the road would only attract his attention. So she just kept walking toward him. As she got closer she saw that he was one of the young men from the back of the van, this one in jeans, a light desert-camo jacket and a red-and-blue baseball cap, with a reddish goatee. He looked very cold. He was hunched, almost doubled over, and hugging himself.

Ru walked a little faster as she approached him. He was closer to the bank than the water, trying to avoid as much of the wind as he could, so she angled as far the other way as she could decently get without appearing totally afraid of him.

When she was nearly abreast of him, he straightened a little, took a couple steps in her direction, attempted a smile, and yelled "Hi!"

She ignored that, as any solitary woman would, she felt, and kept on going, just short of a lope.

He fell in behind her, trying not very successfully at first to keep up. "Hey, you! I said *hi!*"

"Hi," she yelped back, over her shoulder. He broke into a clumsy run then, and she took off at a pace she knew she could keep up for a mile, at least. As the effort warmed him, though, his speed increased, and he narrowed the distance between them. She knew he would catch her pretty soon: a woman in fairly good shape, but also nearly fifty, didn't stand much of a chance against a decently athletic male not much past twenty, with vices that weren't slowing him down much yet....

She chose to slow imperceptibly before she was quite out of breath, and when he was almost close enough to attempt a lunge and a grab, she dug in both feet, swung around, brought her right knee up as hard as she could between his legs, while slamming the roll of quarters she'd been gripping in her pocket even harder against his left temple, round end first.

Somehow she kept her balance, but he went down like a felled redwood. Kneeling, and distastefully, she went through his pockets, finding a cell phone, a greasy wallet mostly full of pornographic photos, an almost-empty pack of cigarettes and a Bic. One at a time, she heaved them all as far as possible into the waves. The cigarettes floated briefly, but nothing else did.

He still hadn't moved, and she wasn't about to kneel beside him again to check for a pulse. She just hoped she hadn't killed him....

—Now what? Clearly, he was, or had been, a sentry. What were they up to, farther along the beach? She didn't have to walk much farther to hear gunfire. The wind carried the flat *crack!*s, half a dozen at a time, along the water's edge.

33

What would Casey do at *this* point? Probably head for home—or for the Djokics' home, more likely, now that she knew what they were up to, and could guess that there wouldn't be anyone back there on Willowbrook but that lame-brained daughter-in-law and the kids. There was certainly no sense in proceeding along the Atlantic here until they spotted her. If Camo was ever going to wake up again he'd be doing it pretty quickly, and even if he wasn't, they might be sending someone back here to take his place soon, so he could have his turn at whatever they were up to. Any way you shuffled and dealt it, she'd better be making herself scarce....

The quickest way to do that, she decided after a dozen more steps, would be to scramble up the slope to the road. She'd make much better time along the shoulder up there. She waited until she got back to where she'd first encountered Camo, and walked backward in his larger steps until she got to where he'd trampled a big patch of sand with his shivering circles. Then she leaped as far as she was able, up into the dry sand that didn't take tracks, and scrambled up to the road from there.

She'd scarcely climbed over the guard rail when a car approached from the Jones Beach direction, behind her. She would have ignored it, but it slowed and stopped beside her. When she looked over, she saw it was a US Parks Ranger in a small white sports car; she couldn't tell what kind.

He lowered the passenger-side window and called out, "What are you doing out here in this weather, Miss?"

"I was just walking along the shore. Clearing the cobwebs out of my brain. When I got sick of the wind, I decided I'd make better time back to my car up here."

"And where's your car?"

"Not much more than half a mile this way, I guess. There was a little place to pull off—"

"You didn't notice the sign that said 'No Parking'?"

"No, I truly didn't. Was there one?"

"There used to be one. I haven't noticed it lately, to be honest. Hop in, I'll drop you there."

She did, and even though he was clearly a decade, maybe more like two, her junior, that didn't keep him from asking, rather sweetly, if she'd like to stop in Oak Beach for a nice hot cup of coffee.

"What time is it?" she asked, as if she were considering his offer. "Almost four already? Omigod, thanks, but I've got to get home before my kids do!"

✣

Passing through Oak Beach again, Ru spotted the van and the Hummer parked side by side, Djokic the Younger behind the wheel of the van, with a newspaper propped against it. He didn't look up.

By the time she got to Babylon, she'd decided she'd never make it back to Brooklyn without a meal under her belt. And just like an answer to one of those Yiddish prayers she never had to learn, a gleaming kosher deli/restaurant appeared out of the setting sun. She ordered the comfort food of her barely remembered grandmother's kitchen: matzo-ball soup, hot corned beef on rye and an enormous dill pickle, with a celery soda. The food came within five minutes of the waitress taking her order, and she ate fast. By the time she finished, she felt ready for anything.

Before and after she'd ordered, while she ate, and driving back through the early, neon-sprinkled night, she tried both of Bob's phone numbers, left urgent messages for him to call her, and debated her options. Even going it alone, this might well be the best opportunity that would ever present itself to see if Casey was in the Djokics' attic. The question was, how much time did she have? How soon would the others have discovered Camo, or heard from him, if he'd recovered sufficiently to communicate? What would their reaction be? They could have no idea where she came from, or where she went; would they spend time searching for her along Ocean Parkway, or head directly for home?

It didn't matter, she decided. None of it—this was her big chance, and she had to try, with or without Bob....

34

Bob stood on the third step for five minutes by his watch and, hearing nothing suspicious, moved to the fourth, then the fifth. The sixth step creaked even louder than the third had, but he only waited ten seconds there before proceeding on up.

The whole space was open, and unfinished, with uncovered windows at either end that let in enough light from the streetlights and xmas illumination in the neighborhood to make the flashlight superfluous. There were three chimneys emerging from below and passing through the roof, but from where he stood, Bob could clearly see that Casey was not presently attached to any of them. He examined each of them closely, though, to be certain that no one had ever been chained to them in the manner he was sure he had been, somewhere. His conclusion was: Definitely Not.

There wasn't much else up there, but there was a stack of

bundles of asphalt roof shingles, knee-high and six or eight feet back from the front window that faced across the street. Bob sat down there, once he'd divested himself of his utility belt, and freed both his canteen and a granola bar from it. He'd had two hits on the one and chewed and swallowed most of the other before he remembered his cell phone was in his pants pocket, turned off since he'd left the pickup. There were five messages from Ruby, he saw right away, but before he could play any of them, another call came through:

"Hello? Bob? Are you there?"

"Hi, Ruby? What's up?"

"Plenty! Where are you?"

"You'll never believe it—in the attic across the street from the Djokics', looking down at their xmas tree. Where are you?"

"About three blocks from there. Can you meet me out in front?"

"Gimme two minutes—no, better make it three."

"I'll park around the corner until I see you cross the street. Wait at the curb, I'll pick you up there, and we'll drive to their side door."

"Gotchya!"

"Oh, and we're cops, all right?"

"Whatever you say, m'Dear!"

✠

On the way down both sets of stairs, Bob decided not to worry about the ladders on the back fence, and went straight out the front door, leaving it unlocked. Never burn your bridges until you have to, was one of his mottoes. Even so, Ru was already parked at the curb in front of the Danovs' and climbing out of her car.

"Changed my mind," she said, and added somewhat cryptically, he thought: "In case we get interrupted…." As they hurried up the driveway to the side entrance, she attempted to explain: "They're all out on Ocean Parkway...." By then she was leaning on the bell. They both heard it pealing inside.

Finally Shannon approached, asking timidly: "Who is it?"

That flummoxed Ruby; she'd hoped the woman would look out and recognize her; she was willing to trade on Shannon's misconception—that she, Ruby, was a cop, because she had accompanied Detective Thomas—but she was not up to flat-out claiming to *be* an officer, which she knew to be a serious crime. Bob, however, suffered under no such compunction.

"Open up! Brooklyn police! Make it snappy!" he yelled.

Shannon was already fumbling with the locks by the time he'd finished his outrageous lie, and once she'd glimpsed Ruby, she opened wide. She was in a dressing robe with a big-eyed, snot-nosed two-year-old in her arms. However, "I was told ya gotta show me a warrant," Shannon protested in the same whiny voice.

"We can do that," Bob said loudly, "we can go back and pick up the god-damned warrant—but if we do, lady, we're coming back with a *squad* of cops, and we'll tear this whole place apart!"

"Oh, no! No, we don't want that!"

"Good for you! What we have to do won't take ten minutes, then we'll be out of your hair...." By then he was all the way in the door, headed for the front of the house, where he figured he'd find the main staircase, with Ru right on his heels and Shannon trailing querulously.

"Whatchya lookin' for?" she wanted to know.

"Just a quick peek in your attic, missus," Bob assured her, "then we're gone!"

"No!" Shannon cried, as the child in her arms began to cry in earnest, "come back when my husband's here"—and she grabbed Bob's sleeve desperately.

They were all at the head of the stairs by then, too jammed together for any of them to move forward. Bob solved that problem by shifting back down a step, creating enough space for Ru to slip by him. "That first door, go!" Bob told her, pressing his flashlight in her hand and pointing at the door it would've been if he were still across the street, while Shannon tried to seize both his arms without dropping her now-shrieking child. Then she suddenly realized what Bob had strapped under his left arm, and would've tossed the suddenly frantic two-year-old on its head, if Bob hadn't managed a spectacular catch. And now she forgot all about the gun, trying to grab her child back—who wasn't having any of it, and clung to Bob's holster harness for dear life.

Bob was wrong, the door he'd indicated covered a full-to-bursting linen closet, but the next one Ru turned to held steps leading up into darkness. She groped at the walls on either side to no effect, then took two backward steps and looked on either side of the door. There were four switches in a panel on the right, and it was the third switch she flicked. She took the dusty stairs two at a time.

35

There was only a single forty-watt bulb dangling from the peak of the roof where the stairs culminated in the middle of the attic floor, and both ends of the house were shrouded in complicated shadows thrown by heaps of cardboard boxes and furniture. Since she happened to face that way, Ru dashed toward the chimney toward the rear of the building, calling "Casey! Are you here?"

She stumbled over something low and heavy, fell, and scarcely paused to get her legs underneath her again. Blindly, she ploughed into the chimney's rough cement surface, and felt her way around all four sides.

No Casey.

But there was still the chimney at the other end! She was up again and running that way almost before she'd finished the thought. She paused under the light bulb at the middle of the attic when Bob shouted up the staircase:

"Is he there?"

"Not done looking yet!" she replied, and charged forward, only to trip and fall again, full-length and quite painfully this time, into a noisy pile of boxed glassware. On her feet once more and not too cut up, she hoped, she moved more cautiously the rest of the way to the chimney at the front of the house.

And there was no one there, either.

At last she remembered the flashlight Bob had thrust in her hands, switched it on, and poked its beam around, before and behind her, until she had to admit:

No, Casey really wasn't up there....

✣

Shannon sat crouched on the top step of the flight between the living room and the bedroom floor with her child on her knees, both of them too curious to be frightened anymore.

"What was ya expectin' to find up there?" Shannon asked. "I never go up there, myself. It's too creepy, even in the daytime."

"Look, we made a mistake, we're very sorry, and now we're leaving, okay?" Ru said. "We won't trouble you any more."

—We'd better be leaving, she thought. That crew in the van and the Hummer could show up any minute....

As if he were reading her mind, Bob set a mighty pace, down the staircase and back through the house to the door where they'd entered. He was waiting on the driveway when Ru called over her shoulder, "Thank you, Missus Djokic, goodbye!" and began to pull the door closed behind her.

Then stopped, and froze for a moment, looking up, ahead.

There was one chimney, the same size, color and design as the ones on the house, protruding from the center of the garage roof.

Ru reopened the door and poked her head back inside. Shannon, the child dangling over her shoulder, was making tracks for the kitchen.

"Ma'am? Just one more thing, please. We might be in big trouble when we get back to the station if we haven't been completely thorough. You know how those things go. They could even send someone else back out here. If you would just let us have a peek in that apartment up there...."

"No, that's Mister Djokic's! I couldn't—he doesn't let anyone up there"—

"Just one peek. Please! And then you'll never see us again, I promise! You must have keys...."

Shannon shook-nodded yes, then no, then looked away irresolutely, meanwhile avoiding at all costs a glance at a board full of keys hanging beside the doorway where Ru stood. One ring had a label above it that said "GAR – GAR APT." Ru grabbed it and ran for the door where Bob was already waiting.

36

The side door to the garage opened onto a small vestibule, facing another door that would necessarily lead into the garage itself, with a second on the right that revealed a staircase up to the apartment. Neither was locked, but the metal-sheathed door at the top of the stairs was, and required two complicated keys.

The apartment was very Spartan: there was a tiny, immaculate kitchenette, a long table set against the wall with two large maps pinned up above it of Brooklyn and the Balkans, a big steel desk with a computer on it, a row of olive-green filing cabinets, a rather small TV with chairs and a short couch gathered around it, photos of chummy, suntanned men with big black mustaches holding lots of guns pinned or propped up everywhere, and a large flag hanging on another wall that Ru guessed must be Croatian.

There was a row of three doors on the far walls, which opened onto a bedroom on either side and a bathroom in the middle, all three both Spartan and immaculate. Access to the attic was through the ceiling of the slightly larger bedroom, on the left. There was a trap door painted white to match the ceiling, and a step-ladder that unfolded down at the yank of a cord. Bob yanked the cord. Ru was upstairs before the bottom step hit the floor, at least in Bob's estimation, again with his flashlight in her hand but this time with full awareness of it....

"What do you see?" Bob wondered.

"Wait, let me—" and then all he heard from above was her running feet and an inarticulate cry.

"I'm coming up," Bob called, and when he got no reply, that's what he did, Glock in hand. But without his flashlight he couldn't see much. Oh, he could see the flashlight beam drawing doodles on the roof and rafters, and some vague commotion beneath, but it wasn't until he'd crossed nearly half of the attic that he could make out what that rotating white thing was: Ruby uncoiling sticky gauze from Casey's head.

"Don't take it all off!" Bob yelped.

"Why the hell not?" they both wanted to know.

"Because I took mine off all at once, 'n' even if it was after dark, my eyes near killed me for hours. Get used to it like that, then take a little more off, and so on."

"Sounds smart," Casey admitted, grinning horribly.

—Christ, he looked, and smelled, terrible. He was incredibly filthy. Or so Bob quickly realized, but then, he'd cleaned himself up after half as much time spent here, and knew how much dirt *he'*d collected. Ru didn't seem to notice, even with Casey lying in her lap, his head hugged to her breasts.

"Ruby, can I have the flash?" She didn't react when Bob drew it out of her hand. He stepped to the opposite side of the chimney and soon found that the chain was held together back there by an open padlock. Disengaging it, he said, "We better get out of here," just as both he and Ruby heard two garage doors rolling open beneath them, then gunned engines, door slams, loud male voices, and heavy footfalls on the lower stairs.

"Well, it *was* a good idea—getting out of here, I mean."

"Yeah, wasn't it…."

"…Did we redo both locks on that door at the top?" Bob whispered.

"I know *I* didn't," Ru said.

"Nor I," Casey croaked, just getting his voice back from that lengthy speech a moment ago.

"Very funny," Ru couldn't help saying, while Bob breathed an "Oh-oh," and then, as they heard feet and voices immediately below but no sort of alarm, sheepishly: "I guess I must've done it without thinking…."

"What about the bedroom door, did we close it?"

"I think so."

"And the stairs and trap door?"

"Nope!" both she and Bob said as they streaked as silently as possible back in that direction. The steps came up quietly enough, but the door made a slight bang as it closed against the ceiling. Apparently no one down there was disturbed, though, and no one had looked into the bedroom yet....

—But they could be coming up at any time to feed, etcetera Casey, both thought at once, and they crept back to where he was.

"Gotta chain you up again, Pal," Bob whispered. "Don't know if you heard, but they're back, and could be coming up here."

"I heard," Casey whispered back. "I'm hearing a lot better now, with less gauze, and I reached up under it and took my dead ha-ha's out—will you please hang onto them, Ru?"

"Ha-ha's?"

"He means his hearing aids," Ru told Bob, zipping them into an inside jacket pocket. "That's what I always call them, so as not to embarrass him in public. The batteries must've quit."

"Uh...that's great. That gauze better go back, too, don't you think?"

"Aren't we going to jump them as soon as they come up?"

"If you say so. What do we want to do to them?"

"Nothing loud or lethal," Ru said. "They'll be our hostages, won't they, for a safe passage out of here?"

"Sounds like as good a scheme as any to me...."

✛

They took positions on either side of the accordioned stepladder and waited for pizza time. Bob gave Ru his five-inch knife and the tear gas capsule he always carried on his key chain, keeping the Glock for himself, and also the frontal position. He put Ruby farther back in the shadows, opposite the way anyone climbing up would be facing.

They didn't have long to wait, but it certainly seemed long, and while they waited, Bob discovered he was standing next to a roughed-in sink and toilet with three stud walls around them, sheet-rocked only on the inside. The fixtures must be directly over the ones in the bathroom on the floor below, he thought, and that made sense—it was the most cost-efficient place to put them. But why were they up here in the attic at all? That didn't make sense—unless they were added later, just to accommodate keeping prisoners up here....

The whole group down below was discussing something intensely for at least a quarter-hour. Then, as the talk tailed off, some one, quite possibly plural, tramped back down the flight of stairs. Only then did they hear somebody else enter the bedroom directly below them and yank on the cord.

As the steps unfolded downward, an inverted pyramid of light shot upward, causing both Bob and Ruby to back up a couple yards in order to stay in complete darkness. Two heads appeared, one at a time, then shoulders. The set that came first was one Ru hadn't seen before: it was another ear-ringed skinhead, this one in a hooded orange sweatshirt, the hood thrown back exposing big ears and a fat neck, with a machine pistol gripped in his right hand. Below and behind him came Camo, carrying a paper sack. So she hadn't killed him after all, Ru realized, with a mixture of relief and regret....

Bob waited until the two had both moved away from the ladder and turned in Casey's direction before stepping into the light, almost at their elbows, in the classic two-handed cop-crouch. "Freeze, mammy-jazzers," he said in a hair-raising whisper, "and you, let go of that Uzi now, or you're both very suddenly dead."

Ru, from behind, already had both hands on the gun Bob had now supplied a name for, and she took full possession of it as the chubby kid's arms went skyward, unbidden. She swung automatically toward Camo as he half-turned in her direction. She had no idea how to fire the thing, but she gave a very realistic impression of willingness to do so, and Camo imitated his buddy, so fast he dropped the stale pizza bag, which fortunately didn't make much noise as it hit the floor.

"Keep walking in that direction, bozos," Bob said quietly now, "hands behind your heads, and pray hard you don't stumble."

37

Bob securely tied Camo's and Chubby's hand behind their backs with short pieces cut from his fifty-foot line, ordered them to sit on opposite sides of the chimney as soon as Casey was freed from there again, then gagged them both with the gauze from Casey's head.

"Are you ready for me to take it all off?" Ru asked him. When Bob raised his eyebrows significantly, she added, "I mean the gauze!"

"I think so." Casey said. "Just don't shine that flashlight in my direction for a while."

Bob used the chain next, to pin their hostages in place. "We ought to get back to the ladder," he told Ru. "Casey, you better stay here, keep an eye on these two, okay?""

"Fine with me, if I can use that john first, and drink a bunch of water. I don't feel very useful yet, I must confess."

"You might try washing your hands and face, too."

"An excellent idea...."

They left the ladder extended and the trap door hanging, taking up positions on either side as close as they could get without moving into the light. Bob took the Uzi, and soon familiarized himself with its simple workings, also making sure that it was loaded. He gave Ru a quick mimed lesson in firing the Glock: grip it with both hands, aim low, the safety's already off....

After twenty minutes more by Bob's watch, someone else came into the bedroom and called up: "Hey, Ivo? What's the holdup?" When he got no answer, he put one foot on the bottom step, and Bob grinned toothily, guessing they were going to take another hostage, but whoever it was seemed to think better of proceeding alone, and retreated to the bedroom doorway where he hollered: "Hey, there's no answer up there!"

"So go up 'n' check it out, dork!" a voice yelled back.

"Bullshit. Why don't you?"

"We better call Boris," another voice said, and when nobody argued, "I'll do it then, okay..." They heard, but couldn't understand, a very brief phone call, then "He'll be right over. Let's try to look like we got all our shit together here, okay?" Then chairs scraping, and TV noise clicked off, and boots on the stairs below. More voices, lower, indecipherable. Then nothing but silence until a voice directly beneath the trapdoor called loudly:

"Ivo? Larry? Where are you guys?"

More silence, then: "Who's up there?" And still more silence, until the light in the bedroom went off, and the door closed immediately afterward, taking all the light with it.

Ten minutes elapsed. Then they heard the door open again, but it didn't let much light into the room or up into the attic now. Bob readied his infrared glasses....

The ladder creaked. Then complete silence for more than a minute. Then a creak at a different pitch. And silence, until Bob said: "Okay, stay right there. No more up, no down. Or I'll blow your fucking—I said *stay right there*. I can see you just fine, asshole— and you can't see me right now, because I'm at your back—don't try turning around, either—and I mean both of you, goddamn it!"

Ru found it frustrating not to be able to see what was going on, but she couldn't even determine exactly where the hole in the floor was. All she knew was she'd better stay put, shut up, and let Bob run the show. She just hoped he wouldn't do anything too wild....

"Now—keep those weapons pointed down—" Bob began, just as a gun somewhere close fired a short burst. Ru saw an instant's flash of vertical light near where she'd last seen Bob, who continued calmly while her ears were still ringing: "...and tell whoever just tried to hit me through the ceiling that if anyone pulls any trick like that again, I'll blow both your fucking heads off. *Is that clear?*"

Mutters of agreement, then more silence.

"Okay. Now both of you, hand up those Uzis. Upper Guy, reach up here and put yours on the floor, as far over as you can. Lower Guy, pass yours up, and Upper Guy again, put it beside yours...good. Now resume climbing, but go slow, and keep your hands where I can see 'em...stop right there, you, and you stop right beside him. Both of you, take those glasses off and hold 'em straight out in front of you...."

Ruby didn't have to be told to collect them, or to put on the first pair she manage to grope. Some night vision had returned to her by this time, and she was able to circle behind Bob to get over there, without risk of falling into the hole. Vision through the glasses was strange, reminding her of looking at certain Japanese cartoons, but adequate enough for knowing where things were and how to navigate. Everything was a murky black and white, with a pinkish or greenish glow....

"Straight ahead, bozos, and put your hands on your heads," Bob said, "and remember, no sudden moves if you plan on staying alive," while signaling Ru to stay behind and watch the ladder.

38

Ru stood there hoping no one else would be foolhardy enough to climb the steps, and nobody was, apparently. Then suddenly the lights came on out in the big room down below, flooding the bedroom below and that end of the attic with light again. Then an angry voice called, "Dad? What the hell's going on here, anyhow? Did I hear a gun go off just now? You want the neighbors calling the cops?"

"Sorry, Dimitri, it was just an accident. Nobody hurt."

"Well, I hope that's all it was, and you better not have another one. What *is* going on? Why were all the lights out?" At this point someone quietly closed the bedroom door, and Ru couldn't hear anymore.

Bob returned to her side a few minutes later. "All four partridges in the pear tree," he said cheerfully. She told him in a whisper what had been going on. "So Junior's not a party to this prisoner business," he speculated. "That could be a real bargaining chip."

"I thought so, too," Ru said. "Meanwhile, shouldn't we take

advantage of the diversion to pull up the drawbridge?"

"Great idea. Cover me while I do it...." Whatever that meant; she stood where she was, gun pointed downward, while he pulled up the folding steps and the trap door.

From the other end of the attic they could hear the continued buzz of conversation below for several minutes, then the apartment door closing and steps receding down the staircase: it had to be the son who was leaving, they figured.

Casey was wearing the second confiscated pair of infrareds now, and cradling the third Uzi in his arms. He was also munching stale pizza with his free hand. "Anybody else?" he asked, offering the paper bag around. Ruby and Bob both declined.

"I think Boris has been treating us as a training opportunity so far," Bob whispered after a while. "From now on they'll probably be a great deal more careful. But I think we'd better keep a closer eye on that trap door than we're doing at the moment."

He double-checked their hostages before they went back to that end. He'd only been able to get the chain once around all four of them, but with their arms bound behind them, there didn't seem to be much mischief they could get into. He'd used his knife to cut one of the sleeves off Chubby's sweatshirt for mouth-stuffers and to divide up the tape to wrap their mouths shut. A very neat job, if he did say so himself, which he was sorely tempted to do, but didn't....

✣

"...What time is it, Bob?" Ruby wondered after what seemed like a rather long time of nothing happening below, so far as they could tell.

He poked his watch and whispered back, "A quarter past eleven. Time sure flies when you're having fun, don't it?"

"This is your idea of fun?" Casey asked him.

"I haven't had so much since the pigs ate my little brother."

"To paraphrase Jules Feiffer."

"Oh, yeah? He said that first?"

"Well, he printed it first, in *Sick, Sick, Sick*, back in the early 'sixties."

"No kiddin'. I learn something new everyday."

"Shut up, you two—I thought I just heard something," Ru said, as the cord was jerked below and the trap door dropped, releasing the cone of light again and blinding Casey. They'd all been sitting down and now scooted back, away from the hole.

"Hello up there? Are you ready to discuss this situation?"

"Who the hell are you?" Bob asked.

"That doesn't matter—"

"The fuck it doesn't! We talk to Boris Djokic, and nobody else!"

"...Okay, I'll get him."

In the attic, Bob whispered, "Is it all right if I do the talking?"

"You've been doing fine so far," Casey said.

"If I don't like something, I'll poke you," Ruby told him. "And then we stop to consult."

"Fair enough...."

From down below, a deeper voice said, "I am Boris Djokic. And who are you?"

"We're just some folks you shouldn't've fucked with. I think you must know that by now."

"I'm not so sure as you, what I know and what I don't know. I do know you're up there, and this is the only way out. What's more, we have you out-gunned and out-numbered."

"Like shit you do! Besides yourself, you've only got two kids left! And you don't dare use your guns, or your son will have a fit, and your neighbors will call the cops!"

There wasn't any answer to that. Ru tugged Bob's sleeve and

whispered: "So what's our demand? We leave these guys up here, unharmed, if he—"

"Nope, we gotta take three of 'em with us, for shields!"

"I couldn't handle a shield," Casey said. "Don't know if I can negotiate that ladder or stand all that light down there, either."

"Two shields, then. And we'll get you down there somehow. You can keep your eyes damn near shut. You just have to keep that grease gun pointed, and look like you're ready to use it." When Bob heard no further objections, he asked, "Are we all agreed, then?"

"…I'm not sure I can manage with one of those guys as a shield, either," Ruby confessed.

"Sure, you can."

"What if he tries to take this gun away from me?"

"You shoot him."

"I don't think I can."

"You certainly looked like you could, with that first pair. Look like that again, and you won't have to. And once we're down there, just stay behind him. We don't want the others to know one of us is a woman, or they'll take you for our weak link and maybe try something."

"I'll show them who's the 'weak link'!"

"That's the attitude! So, agreed?"

"Looks like," Casey said.

"Okay. *Hey, Boris? Here's how it's gonna be!*"

39

Boris Djokic took his time to reply, but clearly, any sense of initiative he'd held before was missing. "What do you want, then?"

"You know goddamned well what we want—we want *out* of here! And nobody hurt. This is how it's gonna work: You're all clearing out of that bedroom, leaving the light on, and shutting the door. We'll tell you when we're ready to come out. You'll all three be sitting down, in plain sight and facing us, somewhere in the middle of that big room there. I know we can't expect you not to be armed, but I want your guns in plain sight, and not pointed at us. We're going to walk slowly past you, out the door and down the stairs. Nobody else moves, nobody gets hurt. Is that perfectly clear?"

"What about our men you've taken?"

"They'll be up here waiting, all safe and sound."

"How can we be sure you haven't cut their throats?"

"You wanna hear 'em? I'll get 'em singing four-part harmony before we come down, okay? Better still, is there a Croatian anthem?"

"Yah."

"Do they know it?"

"Yah."

"Then I'll get them singing that, so you'll know it isn't us. Now clear out of that room, leave the light on like I told you, and shut the door. We'll tell you when we're ready to come out, okay?"

"Okay."

⁜

"He seemed awfully meek and obedient," Casey said after a minute while they all caught their breath.

"Didn't he, though?" Ru agreed.

"He's got something tricky going through that twisted Balkan brain of his, no question," Bob said, "and whatever it is, we've got to be ready for it. He wasn't called the Whatever-It-Was of Unpronounceable for nothing."

"Do you mind my asking, how do you get 'ready for it' if you don't know what 'it' is?" Ru said.

"Heraclitus did some work on that conundrum," Casey contributed.

"You mean where he says 'You should always expect the Unexpected,' or something like that? I heard a philosophy prof at NYU gnaw that bone for forty-five minutes," Bob inserted, "and didn't get fuckin' Word One. Never, before or after, have I heard such unrelieved gibberish."

"Then let's not contribute further to it," Ru said, for a guaranteed closer.

"...What he said about time being a river, you can't step in it twice, I think that's good stuff," Casey couldn't help saying.

"There's no 'time' in there," Bob insisted. "He just says you can't step in the same river twice. Period."

"The river is *time*," Casey insisted back. "That's why you can't step in it twice—"

"What did I say?" Ru said, and this time it worked. After half a minute, she spoke again:

"Now, gentlemen—do we have a plan?"

✢

There was only one space in the bedroom below that couldn't be seen from the attic: inside the big built-in clothes closet. Three men could easily hide in there, which caused Bob to decide that Ru should be the one to descend the stepladder first. Casey didn't like that, but Bob argued that he was much the best of them, all around, with guns. If Bob saw that closet door open by an inch—he checked: it was shut tight now—he would riddle it, side-to-side, high and low....

Once Ruby was down there safely, Bob would hand her Casey, then the two prisoners they'd chosen to use as shields, and he'd come last. The minute Bob hit the floor, he'd grab his hostage and be out the door, he said, surprise being the best advantage they could ask for, then Ru would emerge to his left with her shield, and Casey should bring up the rear, looking as menacing as he was able.

"You're talking to a more-than-sixty-year-old pacifist, you know," Casey protested. "Who hasn't had a decent meal or the minimum amount of liquid for a fortnight, let alone any restorative sex with his glorious wife—"

"Oh, shut up! You must be the only man alive today who would pronounce it 'fortnit,' you nitwit. And you, Bob: hearing you referring to human beings as shields—as nothing *but* shields—disturbs me, slightly. Also, I think you're taking on much too much all by yourself. You don't have to prove anything to us—we know how brave and smart you are. But the point, right now, is Get Us All Out Of Here Safely. Right?"

"You got a better plan?" Bob looked grim, pure Barrone.

"I wasn't criticizing your plan, Bob. Just trying to improve on it."

"Uh-huh. How about we just get started, & you tell me about those improvements as they occur to you along the way, all right, Ruby?"

"Almost perfect. There may not be, by then, a good moment for you to listen to them."

"True enough," Casey said, poking both of them. "But not to be too Zen about it, let's just *do it*!"

40

There was no one in the closet, and everybody made it down the ladder without making too much noise. Bob grabbed Chubby in a sort of half-nelson, swung him around in front of himself, and threw open the bedroom door.

Boris Djokic and his two students were all seated, just as Bob had instructed, near the TV set. The students, in fact, even seemed to have been watching something on it. They both had Uzis in their laps, and Boris held a Colt forty-five automatic loosely in his hand, resting on the arm of his upholstered chair. The younger men seemed surprised to see Chubby and then, a moment later, Camo, but none of them moved.

"That's real nice," Bob said, showing them the barrel of his machine pistol beside Chubby's arm and beginning to move sideways toward the door at the far end of the room. "Just stay the way you are, and everything'll be ginger-peachy...."

Ru followed, staying as hidden as she could behind Camo, who seemed entirely willing to do whatever she required, and Casey came last, both hands on his Uzi, which was aimed more or less in the right direction, but his eyes were slit and focused on his feet: the last thing he wanted to do was trip and go sprawling....

The room was at most forty feet long, but it felt like at least forty yards. As he approached the door, Bob searched everywhere, with eyes and mind, for the surprise he was sure was in store for them. Nothing he could see seemed suspicious, and how could they pull off any surprises, when all three of them were safely seated in plain sight in the middle of the room? There was only one place, he decided, where a surprise could be hidden—but what could it be?

He stopped when he reached the door and moved to the left, the side that opened, waiting for Ru and Casey to catch up. When they got there, he motioned them to the right, where the hinges were, and clear of where the door would swing open.

"Keep those three back there well covered," he whispered. "Anyone brings his gun up, don't wait, don't hesitate, just shoot them all. And just ignore whatever happens over here—" as he reached for the handle, gave it a twist, and threw open the door as fast and hard as it would go. Almost at the same time he shoved Chubby into the doorway, where another, well-muscled young man came lunging into the room from the landing outside with a bayonet-fixed rifle which missed Chubby's gut by a cat's whisker but went through his right forearm, the one in the remaining sleeve, leaving a shallow but ragged and nasty wound.

"Drop it!" Bob yelled, pressing the barrel of his Uzi into the young man's neck, just below and behind the ear. The rifle was dropped with a clatter and a shriek, as the well-gagged Chubby collapsed beside it like bloody laundry on the floor.

"Quick!" Bob told Ru and Casey, as he stepped back, out of their way, "out and down, I'll cover! And leave him here," jerking Camo out of Ru's grip, and pitching him on top of Chubby, employing the whimpering Rifleman now for his shield.

—Thank Whatever, there's a sturdy handrail, Casey thought, as he took the steps as fast as he dared, gripping the banister at his right side with both hands. Ruby was already at the bottom, watching him come, readying her weapon.

As Bob backed onto the landing, he pulled the door shut behind him. He had the keys Ru had taken from the board in the house already in his hand, the right key forward, and took time to turn that one lock before he high-tailed it down, more a slide than a proper descent, good-foot-first.

"Bring Casey!" Ru told him, "I'll go get my car!" Her keys were where they belonged for once, in the front pocket of her fanny-pack. She had them out before she reached the car, and the engine started before Bob and Casey were a third of the way down the drive, so she swung up there to meet them. As Bob helped Casey into the back seat, shoved the guns in the back with him, and climbed into the front, the house door opened and Dimitri Djokic yelled, "Who the hell are you? Whaddaya think you're doin' in my driveway?"

Ruby gunned it and got out of there fast, but not before Bob had time to yell back, "Go ask your daddy!"

41

"Where'd that seventh bastard come from, that's what I wanna know," Bob wondered as they careened out of Sheepshead Bay, north and westward.

"What he had must've been an SKS, by the way, forerunner to the AK47 and also designed by Kalashnikov; both are fitted for bayonets, and there's tons of 'em in this country.... You're positive, though, that there were only six guys you saw climbing out of the van, out there on the Island?"

"That's all I saw on the ground," Ru corrected. "But I suppose there could've been another guy still inside, giving Boris a hand with those duffels."

"Or he could've shown up here later, on his own, if called," Casey said. "The point is, we didn't really know how many there actually were, we just thought we did, and Boris didn't know we didn't know until you told him that there was only himself and *two* kids left. That gave him his secret weapon. He put his toughest dude out on the landing, to hit us just when we'd think we were home-free."

"And with a deadly weapon he could actually use, because it wouldn't go *bang*! and make Dimitri come running. Pretty clever," Bob said. "There's a lesson here: don't ever tell them anything…."

"Clever, yes, but you outsmarted him," Casey pointed out.

"I knew there had to be a surprise, and I knew it had to be where it was, because there wasn't any other place for it to be—oh, shit!"

"What's wrong?"

"I've got a pickup to pick up and drop off, a front and back door to lock, and a ladder to put back where it belongs—and they're all way back there, ten or twelve blocks, getting farther away, faster and faster!"

"You want me to turn around and go back to Willowlane Brook, or whatever it is? Are you kidding? I have a very seriously undernourished man in the back seat, who needs home-care immediately, if not a hospital—"

"No more hospitals!" Casey cried from behind her head. "If that's what you had in mind, better you had left me there."

"You're not serious. If you were, you wouldn't use such archaic grammar."

"Hey, I love you!" Casey cried now, full of joyous gratitude.

"After tonight, Mister Jones, you had damned well better."

"… Or I could cab back," Bob said to himself, then to Ruby: "There's a major subway stop coming up in three or four blocks, I forget what it's called, but I'll bet there's a cab stand…."

⁜

"…First the tub, then you," Ru said. "I've got enough off you now so you won't ruin the furniture. I'm going to be at least an hour, though, scrubbing that hideous museum piece in there before you're going to get any cleaner in it."

"An hour to clean the shortest tub I've ever been scrunched into, since infancy?"

"It may be short, but you must admit it's deep, as well as dirty."

"All the better to keep coal in," Casey said, in reference to the facts that the building was meant for Irish workmen just off the boat, and originally heated only by a tiny fireplace in the front room and a cast-iron cook stove at the back, and also that landlords back then commonly argued there was no need to supply tubs, their tenants would just use them for coal bins, since the Irish never bathed unless forced.... Casey remembered having had to explain every part of that anecdote when he told it to Ru. Then he'd gone on to ask her the riddle, *What's a wheelbarrow for?* and was stupid enough to tell her the answer: *It gets an Irishman up on his hind legs.* Even convincing her, afterward, that it really was one of Abe Lincoln's favorite jokes did nothing to redeem him. She did not think racial humor was humorous, period.... Here he was, falling asleep, on his feet.

"Go crash in your Lazy-Boy," Ru urged him.

"Great idea. But first I plan to vaporize a little hooty-weed. Want some?"

"Not me. I've got a lot of work ahead of me, first that tub, then you. And I'll probably have to do the tub again, after I scrub you in it."

"Christ, it's good to be home."

"Christ, it's good to have you."

"You haven't had me yet, but you will, you will!"

"Not until you're much cleaner than you are now, I won't. And probably not until you've had a real meal and some real rest. Go on, now—I'm busy!"

When he did attempt to flop down into his Lazy-Boy, Mrrrowski hissed mightily. Ru opened the back window and sternly ordered the cat "Out!"

42

"You know, I think we made a big mistake last night," Ru said the next noon, as they breakfasted on oatmeal with raisins, honey and half and half.

"And what's that?"

"Instead of coming home, we should've gone straight to the police station and turned in those Uzis and told them the whole story."

"Well, I for one am glad we did what we did. I just wish we'd done it faster. I mean getting me clean and fed faster, not what came later."

"But now they won't believe us. They'll say, if that were true, why didn't we go straight to them?"

"They would never believe us anyway, Sweetie."

"Why not?"

"For one thing, I'll bet Bob will insist you leave him out of the story entirely. And how are you going to get them to believe you freed me single-handedly?"

"Why would Bob insist on that?"

"Okay, say he didn't; you'd still have to explain how the two of you got three Uzis away from them, and took four hostages, without a pretty serious weapon of your own to begin with."

"But we did have a weapon, Bob did—his...rhymes with cock."

"Glock. That's what he won't let you mention. Because I'm sure he has no license to go carrying that thing around."

"Oh...so what are we going to do?"

"I know what I'm going to do: I'm going to catch up on fluids, on eating, and on making love to you."

"That's very nice, but what about the guns? How do we get rid of them?"

"I suggest we just turn them over to Bob. He'll think of something."

"I'm sure he will. Like giving them to deeply disturbed teenagers."

"I'll have to tell him that—no, no, I'm only kidding! Put that spoonful of oatmeal back in the bowl! Please don't start something that you won't get to finish—"

"I won't, huh? I *won't*?"

"Of course you will. I apologize."

"So we've settled the gun question, I guess. What about the Djokic Gang?"

"What about them?"

"Well, we can't just forget about them."

"Why not? That's precisely what I propose to do."

"And just let them...get away with what they did?"

"They didn't exactly get away with it. And I'd be surprised if Boris doesn't lose all or at least most of his disciples, now they've have a taste of the real thing, and seen how ineffective his leadership can be."

"Will they forget about us, though?"

"I'd be very surprised if they didn't. What's in the experience to make them want to remember it? From their viewpoint, it's embarrassment from beginning to end. I don't mean they'll learn anything—the opposite. They'll just forget it—and anyone who brings it up is a jerk."

"Which means they could come on to the idea again—using people at random to teach and learn how to keep a hostage, someone taken prisoner that you've got to hide."

"I don't think Bob and I were quite at random—I sent the cops to their door, and Bob was spying on them. But yeah, I don't doubt that's what they were up to: Gulag Guardsmanship 101-D, concerning appropriate urban revolutionary behavior, specifically kidnapping. I would imagine their primary targets, once they graduate, would be Serbs and Serbian-Americans, at least to begin with. But you never know, do you?"

"I couldn't have said it better myself," Ru told him. "So what do we do about it, if we don't go to the police? Warn the Serbian community?"

"Oooh, that sounds like good fun. If you liked Croats, you're gonna *love* Serbs!"

"Jones—that sounds uncomfortably close to racist."

"I didn't intend it to be more than neutral—what's happened to neutrality, anyhow? How did it acquire such a bad odor? What's wrong with declaring peace one country at a time? Why aren't Sweden and Switzerland admired, instead of snickered at, for their eminently sane decisions to avoid the collective madness of war?"

"Are you trying to change the subject?"

"Of course not—would I do that?"

"You do it all the time."

"Well anyhow, if I were ever to travel to the Balkans, and they weren't currently too heavily involved in doing each other in, I'm sure I could learn to love the land, the food, and almost all the people, of all the different ethnic backgrounds, wherever I went."

"But these are a particular set of really bad guys, whatever their nationality. What do we do about them?"

"There's only one bad guy here, who's scraped together a few—"

"Several."

"You're absolutely right, *several* kids with some Croatian genes in them, probably, and was trying to make them into his own mini-militia, because that's all he knows how to do, and because he doesn't have anything better to occupy him these days."

"You're not saying what Boris Djokic was doing was okay?"

"Of course not. None of it. But you can't stop folks from playing soldier, or anything else they want. Not in any society I'd want to live in.

Until they start doing something like what those jerks were doing to Bob and then to me, and sure, who knows how many victims before us."

"That's what I'm talking about! Exposing them, and stopping them, for good."

"I think they are stopped, those particular nutsos. Boris may recruit some other chumps, but these guys haven't stopped running yet, I'll bet. No matter how dense they might be, they necessarily absorbed one great lesson: whatever you can do to your designated enemies, they can turn around and do it to *you* at least once in a while. This is why armies sometimes dissolve overnight: they learn that lesson en masse...."

"You can't be sure, though."

"Of *course* you can't! Why would you want to be? That way lies totalitarianism. A free society has to take some risks—a lot of risks. Or else turn into a prison state. You went to the proper authorities. Luckily, you ran into some pretty decent individuals, it sounds like. You got nowhere then, when we could've used some help. Now, the best they could offer is complications we don't want. But the likeliest outcome is they'll decide we're pests. If not, if they even begin to believe you, the first thing they'll do is turn the whole problem, and us, over to Homeland Security. Think about it: do you want those jokers putting an oar in?"

"...No...."

"Then let's drop the whole business, and concentrate instead on how indescribably beautiful you are right now."

"I can't go back to bed, Casey. I've got to go to work. You wouldn't believe how far behind you've made me."

"Yes, I would. It's so far another day won't matter...."

✛

When he woke again late that afternoon, Casey walked down to Otto, where Annette greeted him as if he'd never been gone.

"Ruby called me from her office a few hours ago," she explained, "and said you were home, and okay."

"Both very true," he said. "I'm sorry if I've caused you any incon—"

"No, no, that's all right. But I'm afraid you no longer have any choice. I ran out of almost everything I had in her sizes. So I just saved you the nightgown I thought she would like best. Let me see if any of these customers need help, and I'll get it from the back and show you."

It was gorgeous, of course, or rather, he knew Ru would be gorgeous in it. And she, when she tore open Annette's beautiful wrapping job on the morning of the twenty-fifth, told him it was the loveliest negligee he'd ever chosen for her.

43

They couldn't just "drop the whole business," not without giving Bob the gratitude he was due. They invited him over for three-cheese tortellonis in clam, garlic and fresh parsley sauce a week from Tuesday, two days after xmas, when Ru had pretty much caught up with all her most pressing obligations. Just the day before, they'd received a small parcel containing Casey's keys and wallet, with a season's greetings card from the Djokics, bearing the message "Peace on Earth, Good Will to All Men."

"He's reminding us he knows where we are," Ru said grimly, "and that he can always do it again."

"I don't think so," Casey said. "I think it means what it says. He's proposing a truce."

"Hmmph," Ru said. "Don't forget, he's still the Whatever-It-Was from Unpronounceable. You can't trust a truce with somebody like that."

"Well, I'm glad for the wallet and keys. And that I hadn't started the very tedious process of replacing all that stuff yet."

When Bob arrived, forty minutes late and carrying a litre of brandy, he said, "You'll never guess what I got in the mail yesterday."

"Your wallet and keys and seasons greetings from the Djokics."

"…I guess you did, too, then."

"Yep."

"I spent over a week trying to replace all that stuff, and still hadn't got my social security card…. So have you come up with what we should do to him yet?"

"No, have you?" Ru said.

"Nothing," said Casey, flatly.

"*Nothing*? After what he did to us?"

"Short of kidnapping him and holding him blindfolded in an

attic for three weeks, would anything be appropriate?"

"Look, we gotta do something! You can't just let something like that go. It wouldn't be *right*!"

"And what would be? Another grievous wrong?"

"Okay, okay, two wrongs don't make a right, I know, but…it just burns my ass, that's all…."

"If it's any consolation," Ru said, "I agree with you, Bob. I just can't think of what could do it, though. What would really burn *his* ass, and not leave us open to a come-back, or criminal charges."

"That last don't bother me none," Bob said, "but thanks for telling me how you feel, Ruby. I'm sure, between the two of us, we can come up with just the right—"

"And when you do, tell me," Casey said, "and I'll point out what's wrong with it. Meanwhile, I'm cooking the pasta. We eat in five minutes."

✣

Immediately after dinner, Bob attempted to revive the subject, until Casey felt moved to say: "Actually, given who he is, a murderous sociopath who hates everyone and everything non-Croatian, I thought Boris behaved very sanely throughout our encounter. If he continues to behave like that, I'm sure he'll do his best to avoid such encounters in the future, because they're so volatile, with the outcome so unpredictable."

"So you'd just let him go," Bob repeated, "let him do it again, or something worse, if he doesn't continue to 'behave like that'?"

"What's the alternative? You want to start eliminating *potential* malefactors? Who guarantees that's what they are? Besides you?"

"All right, I cede the point. I'm really not happy, though."

"You should be. You pulled off the best-possible conclusion. And with the best possible results: nobody killed."

"I want a confrontation with that shit-head!"

"I think you had one. Or as close as you can come to one with that guy, and come away unscathed...."

Bob left that night an hour later than they both had hoped he would, with more brandy on board than would allow most people to walk, let alone drive, and there was no further word from him until the Thirtieth of January.

44

On the Second of January, a few minutes after Ru got home from work, the doorbell rang.

"Who is it?" she asked the intercom.

"Special Delivery. You have to sign."

"Come to the back door on the right at the end of the hall, then," she said, and then turned to Casey, busy at the stove. "Are you expecting anything?"

"Nope. You're not?"

"I don't think so...."

"Put the chain on then," he suggested, "let him pass it through the crack," but he spoke too late. By the time he'd turned off the burners and divested himself of his New Mexico apron ("The Eternal Question: Red Or Green?"), the fellow was in the door and smoothly seating himself at the oak table opposite Ruby.

"Sorry to be misleading," the man said, with an expression showing no sorrow whatsoever. "I find it the simplest way to gain entrance." He was dressed like a Kansas undertaker. He produced a badge in a leather folder from his breast pocket, offered it to both of them, and put it away again. It wasn't one Casey had ever seen before, but he could guess what it was.

"You're Homeland Security."

"That's right. Or right enough. The title's slightly different."

"And what do you want?"

"Simply verification. Which you can grant by a nod. You sign nothing, you say nothing, you're not committed to anything, and you'll never hear from us again. Understood?"

"Perfectly. So far."

"On or about December Seventh, you were apprehended in front of this building by persons unknown to you, drugged, and conveyed to Twenty-six-thirty-two Willowbrook Lane in the Borough of Brooklyn, New York, where you were held against your will, and kept bound and blindfolded, until December Eighteenth, at which time you were freed by other persons unknown. Is this statement true, in whole or in part?"

"I think you must have the wrong K. C. Jones," Casey answered.

"Please think again, Mister Jones. You have nothing to lose here by telling us the truth."

"But somebody does. Whether it's true or not."

"Why should that bother you, after what they did to you?"

"Maybe it wouldn't, if I *were* the guy you were looking for. But I'm not."

"You're absolutely sure of that, Mister Jones?"

"Absolutely."

"What about you, Missus Jones? Or would you prefer I address you as Miz Schneider? As I understand it, you were somewhat involved as well."

"I never disagree with my husband, Mister...I don't think I caught your name."

"I don't think I gave it. Smith will do. William Smith."

"Well, Mister Smith, I'm very sorry we can't help you."

"So am I. Well, good evening."

"And a good one to you, too.... Is anything over there about to burn, Casey?"

"No, I turned everything off."

"Well, I hope you'll turn everything back on, because I'm starving." Casey stood by the stove again, sputtering. Finally she decided he was laughing. "What's so funny?"

"'I never disagree with my husband'—can I get that in writing?"

"Not in a million years, Mister Jones."

45

"Good news!" Bob said in the message he left on their machine on January Thirtieth. "Too good for the phone! Lemme know when would be convenient, I wanna tell you face to face!"

When Casey called back, he said, "Why don't you come for dinner tomorrow night?"

"Because it's my turn. Meet me at Cucina's at eight o'clock."

"Are you sure you can get a reservation at such short notice? They're really popular, you know."

"I'm sure," Bob said. "They know me."

Bob was at the bar when they got there, not quite ten minutes late. Ru had thought the occasion worthy of a new dress and shoes, so she probably had already spent almost as much as he was going to.

"The table's ready," Bob said, signaling the maitress d'. "Let's go pig out!"

In spite of Bob's urging them to order as he did, Ru and Casey performed their usual number at Cucina: he picked an entrée, and she selected what she hoped would be the lightest pasta dish, and they split half of both, taking the rest home because all the dishes there were enormous. They also split their favorite side dish, escarole with garlic and tomatoes in olive oil. Casey made it at home, but simple as it was, he never could get it to taste as incredible as theirs—it had to be the olive oil, he was certain. She ordered one glass of red, and he had a small bottle of San Pelligrino. Bob ordered an entrée and a pasta dish, and two sides, and dessert, and ate everything before him, with three Gibson martinis. They talked before and after, but not during; all three agreed you don't talk over food that good, not about anything important.

"Good news, like I said," Bob told them at last, "but brief. Bobby got it, don't ask me where. The first fact I can vouch for: Boris Djokic no longer resides at twenty-six-thirty-two Willowbrook Lane. I've driven by a dozen times, the windows over the garage are always dark with the blinds closed. I tried the phone once, and got some cop-type who tried to keep me on the line long enough to trace me. Anyhow, Bobby says he's no longer in the States. His theory is, the Army turned Boris over to the Commission at The Hague. They needed a Crote monster to balance what they've been doing to a few

Serb monsters."

"So Mister Smith didn't take our word for it," Ru said, and then explained to Bob about their mysterious visitor.

"I didn't expect he would," said Casey.

"Why in hell would you ever want to protect that creepo?" Bob demanded.

"I didn't. I just wouldn't ever want to rat anybody out to those Homeland Security creepos," Casey told him.

"Good point," Bob conceded, and downed the last of his martini.

46

Real life has no such things as conclusions, Casey had long believed, but if there was one to this slice of these lives, it began the following October, a year and a third after that day when Casey had started across Prospect Park West on his way to see two Truffaut films in Manhattan. The conclusion commenced with an excited phone call from Bill di Marco's secretary. They finally had a solid court date, she told the message machine: next Tuesday, in the morning sometime, as usual no telling just when. She gave the number of the courtroom, and said, while his presence probably wouldn't be necessary, Casey should try to make it just in case the judge had a question for him, and he should get there as close to nine o'clock as he could.

Since this was the third or fourth time they had received such a call, Casey didn't pay it much attention, but on Monday afternoon there was another call, reiterating everything, saying it was definitely on, and he should do his best to get there.

"Are you going?" Ru asked, when she'd heard the message.

"I wasn't planning on it," Casey told her.

"Are you doing anything else tomorrow morning?"

"Not especially. There's a job on Fourteenth Street I might look at." He'd started taking small jobs again, if they didn't involve any undue strain on his hip.

"I'm not too busy, either. Why don't we both go?"

"You mean, like a date?"

"Sure. I might even buy you lunch, if you win your case, and if you're well dressed enough to take into one of those lawyerly restaurants down there."

"No tie."

"I didn't expect you to wear a tie. I don't think you own one, do you?"

"Of course I do. It's knit, green and yellow, our high school colors, and ties with a Windsor knot as big as my fist."

"So no tie."

"No loafers with tassels, either."

"I know, because you never had any. Even if you did, nobody would ever take you for a lawyer, Casey, believe me. So how about a clean shirt and your one-and-only sport coat?"

"It's a deal," he said, "but I think you should only buy me lunch if I *don't* win. If I do, I should buy *you* lunch, it's only fair."

"…You don't think you're going to win, do you?"

"Well, to be honest, I never have. Lotteries, either. Or poker for money."

"Have you ever bought a lottery ticket? Or played poker for money?"

"Of course not. Do I look that stupid?"

"Only when you smile like that. You know you can't win the lottery if you don't buy a ticket?"

"That probably explains it. By the way, what are we doing tonight, after dinner?"

"What would you like to do, Casey?"

"Guess."

"Not again!"

"Oh, yes, again! And again! And again!"

"Oh, why not. I can't think of anything better...."

"Neither can I—ever."

✢

Tuesday was one of those magical mornings that New York City usually has several of, in May and again in October: cool and clear, windless and full of bright promise. New Yorkers sometimes smile at each other, even at people they don't know, on such mornings.

They took the subway to Borough Hall and strolled the several blocks to the proper courthouse. Finding the right room took a while. Bill di Marco was there, as were dozens of knots of standing, chatting, mostly young, mostly coffee-drinking lawyers, with a scattering of clients, mostly seated, worried-looking. It was nearly ten o'clock. Nothing was happening yet, no judge in sight. When Bill spotted them, he trotted over, grinning confidently, and guided them back out into the hallway for a whispered conference.

"He's supposedly on his way," Bill began, "the judge, I mean. Allstate's here already. I'll point her out to you when we go back in. We're pretty high up on the list, I'm told. We should definitely get called before noon."

"That's good," Casey told him. "I hate a late lunch."

"Aren't you excited?" Bill asked, squeezing Casey's bicep.

"Should I be?"

"Well, sure, after all this time, we're finally going to get a decision! Look, I know this judge pretty well, I mean, I've been up before him something like four or five times. He's fair, and he listens, he really does. I think he'll give my argument his full attention."

"I certainly hope so," Ruby said. Like most of the women hurrying past them, she was wearing a tailored suit, but somehow her suit didn't say "lawyer," not even to Casey's untutored eyes. It said, "some kind of social worker." You can't help learning these distinctions, if you live long enough in places like Park Slope....

After a somewhat awkward pause, Bill said, "Come on back in, I'll show you Allstate." Peering around the room, he pointed out a slender, thin-lipped blonde in a grass-green pant suit who was plucking a tiny cell phone off the strap on her slim black leather briefcase and heading for the hallway they'd just left. She looked scarcely old enough to have finished high school.

Meanwhile, at the far end of the long courtroom, there was a quiet sort of commotion as a heavy-set middle-aged man in a dark brown three-piece suit that screamed "I cost a *pot* of money!" made his appearance through a small side door in the dark wood paneling that ran ten feet high all around the room. A skinny bald man with a notebook cradled in his elbow followed behind as if attached by a very short leash.

"There's the judge," Bill whispered, to no one's surprise. "And the clerk. Now we'll get going."

"I would hope so," Ru said.

The judge and clerk walked past the high bench and sat down behind an ordinary, but large, desk near the back wall.

"They've been working on that bench for more than a year," Bill whispered. "Carpenters have, I mean."

"I don't see anybody working on it," Casey said.

"Well, they can't work on it while court's in session. I guess that's what taking so long."

Just then the blonde in the green pant suit hurried past them, saying, "I just heard we've been bumped up to third place. Are you ready?"

"Of course I am," Bill told her, then to Casey and Ru he said, "I better stick close to her, just in case they bump us up again."

"Can we sit down somewhere?" Casey asked. "My hip hurts."

"That's good," Bill said, then grinned. "I mean, maybe it's a good sign. Uh, better sit out in the hallway, near the entrance so I can find you if I need you, okay?"

They sat on a long low bench out in the hall until a quarter past noon, when Bill appeared with shining eyes, bent down close, and squeezed Casey's shoulder. "I think it went very well," he said. "The judge asked a lot of questions, and that's usually a good sign. It means he hasn't made up his mind yet."

"So no decision?" Ru asked.

"Oh, no. You never get a decision *at* the hearing. We'll get that in writing, in a month or two. Uh, look, I've gotta run, I'm—"

"So have we," Casey said, "we're late for lunch."

"So who buys?" Ru wanted to know as they found their way out of the building, then stepped carefully down tall marble steps where people sat shoulder-to-shoulder, eating their lunches. The smells were wonderful, Casey thought: hotdogs heaped with sauerkraut or onions in tomato sauce, bagels with cream cheese and lox, Italian sausage subs, falafels and tomatoes and chopped lettuce in pita bread dripping yoghurt sauce, mysterious, odorous containers of Chinese, Indian, or Vietnamese takeout.

"I guess we should go Dutch," he said, "how about something off one of these stands along the curb?"

"Oh no you don't, cheapskate," Ru said, and took hold of his elbow. "I want a real meal. There's an excellent French place over on Montague where we shouldn't have to wait more than half an hour for a table."

"And lunch won't be much more than twenty bucks apiece, I suppose, unless you decide to have a glass of wine. Let's grab a hotdog now, to get us there, okay?"

☦

They got the decision the following February, in Bill's office, which had been his father's office. It was a very nice office, wood-paneled, almost like a courtroom.

The decision had gone in Allstate's favor. Which meant, instead of six figures, the check Casey would eventually get would be for barely six thousand.

"I couldn't believe it," Bill said. "I feel really terrible. After all you've been through."

"You don't know the half of what he's been through," Ru told Bill.

"Oh, I do, I saw him in the hospital," Bill said. "Remember? But I mean it, I feel truly awful about this—and … and you know what? I'm not going to take my commission!"

"That's very good of you," Casey told him.

It was easy to tell that Bill thought so, too. He kept his hand clapped on Casey's shoulder all the way to the door.

"Come on," Ru said, running ahead to push the brass-bound ivory button for the elevators. "I guess I owe you an expensive lunch."

"Not necessarily," Casey told her, "not if you're willing to grab a quick sub or falafel, catch the subway to Grand Army Plaza, take a lovely stroll through Prospect Park, and then go jump back into bed with me."

"Is that all you ever think of, Mister Jones?"

"Yes it is, my Dearest Heart. Thanks to you, I feel like a king in this City of Kings, and it's loving you that keeps me alive."

Paul in the 1960s

About the author:

Paul Johnson was a political activist in the 1960s, a founding editor of *WIN Magazine*, and a New Mexico homesteader in the 1970s, who later returned to New York City, where he supported his writing habit with carpentry. In 2001 he settled again in the Southwest, where he lived with his wife, Frances Ciulla, an art therapist. Paul died on November 20, 2006 after a two-year battle with lymphoma. He is sorely missed by his family, friends and many readers. He worked on the final draft of *City of Kings* until the last few weeks of his life. It is his final legacy of words in print.

The Wessex Collective Books in Print

Good fiction does more than tell a story. It gives the gift of experience.

Sandra Shwayder Sanchez. *Stillbird.* From the strangling of a midwife perceived to be a witch in Scotland in the 1880s to thwarted love and the tragedy of incest in West Virginia during the depression thence to Denver on the eve of the sixties, accurate history is enhanced by elements of magical realism in this tale of five generations that is as ancient as the Greek tragedies and as modern as the daily news. ISBN 0-9766274-1-8 $11.00, paper

R. P. Burnham. *Envious Shadows* is a deftly crafted, engrossing contemporary novel, one of those works that is not afraid to face the grim realities of life and the cruelties of society as well as the redeeming power of love... A beautiful work that depicts life in all its grim realities, *Envious Shadows* is a rewarding read. -Mayra Calvani, *Bloomsbury Review* ISBN 0-9766274-2-6 $13.50, paper

Ita Willen. *The Gift.* Meditating upon the seasons in her garden, the author describes in poetic language and penetrating insight how the study and understanding of Buddhism helped her come to terms with the inescapable legacy of the holocaust. Touches of surrealism give this memoir the feel of a novel. ISBN 0-9766274-0-X $11.00, paper

William Davey. *The Angry Dust* tells the story of Prescott Barnes and his family leaving the dust bowl for California, but there its similarities with *The Grapes of Wrath* end. The grandson of a wealthy preacher who disinherited Prescott's father, Barnes, despite his cynical black humor, hostility to religion, and his illiteracy, possesses a fierce integrity and passions that make him larger than life at the same time he is perfectly human. ISBN 0-9766274-3-4 $24.95, hardback

Brian Backstrand's stories from rural America chronicle often small but important moments of the lives of ordinary people. Memories—healing or disruptive, constant or denied—often play an important role in the stories of *Little Bluestem* which link together rural people from various generations caught in the midst of struggle or in a moment of recognition or healing. Backstrand's intention is to lift up ordinary people from rural contexts and place them squarely before his contemporary and often urban readers. ISBN 0-9766274-4-2 $12.95, paper

R. P. Burnham, *On a Darkling Plain*: Samuel Jellerson, 56 and forced into early retirement, is walking in the woods behind the family farm in Maine one fall day when he witnesses a priest molesting a boy. From this one event all the action in the novel follows and draws a wide cross section of the town into a theme that explores the nature of evil and its antidote empathy, the force that creates community, fellow-feeling and a sense of responsibility to others. ISBN 0-9766274-5-0 $12.95, paper

Paul Johnson, *The Marble Orchard.* "...A deep, sweet story of accidental enlightenment... an optimistic coming-of-middle-age novel that will resonate loud and strong with those of us struggling to stay hopeful as we deal with aging, loss, and regrets."–Nancy Cardozo. ISBN 0-9766274-6-9 $18.95, paper

Margaret Guthrie, *The Return.* "Margaret Guthrie's poignant sequel describes the pain of families hiding the actual truth about their youthful experiences from their own children. The story illustrates how traumatic events can ruin relationships. Forgiveness and a 'spiritual' truth touches every member of the community." Minette Riordan, Ph.D., President of Scissortail Publishing. ISBN 0-9766274-7-7 $15.00, paper

Paul Johnson, *City of Kings: The Ongoing Adventures of Casey Jones.* "Like any truly gentle soul, Paul Johnson is at his best writing about mayhem, madness, mystery and murder. Welcome to Brooklyn, but look out: he's in rare form here."–Terry Bisson   ISBN: 978-0-9766274-8-7 $15.00, paper

R. P. Burnham, *The Many Change and Pass.* This novel explores the question of our duty to the earth, which entails this further question: how can we live a decent human life when every individual is part of the many who are transitory and intent upon selfish pursuits that give no thought to what remains after they pass. It begins with the mercury poisoning of a small, impoverished boy and follows Chris Andrews, a ecological activist, Myron Seavey, a progressive librarian, and a dozen other characters as they deal with the implications of this poisoning.   ISBN 978-0-9766274-9-4 $18.95, paper

Sandra Shwayder Sanchez, *Three Novellas: The Last Long Walk of Noah Brown, The King and the Clockmaker, The Vast Darkness.* This collection of novellas is about journeys. In *The Last Long Walk of Noah Brown*, a young man leaves his home in Annapolis in 1965. A complete innocent, he trusts the people he encounters along the roads who give him direction until he settles in New Orleans where he eventually rescues people and animals caught in the flood. *The King and the Clockmaker* examines questions about the genesis of evil, the role of art and the nature of time. In *The Vast Darkness*, a young woman student of anthropology reflects upon the influence of isolated mountain living upon her neighbors. ISBN 978-0-9797516-0-8 $15.00, paper

Wessex books are available from BookLink Distribution (944 Broad Street/ Camden, SC 29020/ Tele: 803-432-5169). Visit them online at the The BookLink Online Store (http://www.thebooklink.com), and under publishers choose The Wessex Collective. For further details, visit the Wessex site at www.wessexcollective.com